Fake Dating

at

Half Moon Bay

Katie O'Connor

Snarky Heart Press

–Fake Dating at Half Moon Bay–
–A Bellamie Brothers of Half Moon Bay Novel–

Published June 2023
Digital ISBN: 978-1-989816-69-1
Print ISBN: 978-1-989816-71-4

Design and cover art by Beck and Dot
Editing by Terri St. Clair

Dedication

For Audrey Carnes.
For inviting me into this project.
And for holding my hand the whole way through.

For Sharon NM.
With great appreciation for your input and suggestions.

For Joanie Wilde.
Thank you for being my mentee,
and for helping me discover more about the writing
process.
This book would not exist without your feedback.
Nor would it exist without your encouragement.
The mentee has become the mentor!

What happens when fake dating turns real?

Confirmed bachelor Zander Bellamie has too much on his plate. He's got a busy veterinary practice to worry about, a mother, three brothers, and a niece who always needs his help. The last thing he needs to add to his life is a girlfriend. Unfortunately, his mother and her friends keep thrusting potential dates in his path. To make matters worse, his brother has hired a new chef. She's bright, pretty, and smart. They click instantly and he can't stop thinking about her.

Heather Olsen is through with men. She just wants to rebuild her life without worrying about another man stealing everything she owns. She's a tough strong woman set on rebuilding her life. She's not about to risk a new job, in a new town, by dating her boss's brother, even if he might be exactly the man her heart is looking for. He's handsome, intelligent, and kind.

Zander is a take charge kind of guy and when he suggests fake dating to get local matchmakers off his tail, Heather is reluctant, but agrees. She's not interested in long term, but fake dating Zander could be her rebound relationship ... the one she uses to test her ability to trust again. When things start to feel real, she doesn't know whether to cut and run, or beg for more. Can they get beyond the reasons they shouldn't be together and forge a love that was meant to be?

Chapter 1

Undulating waves of torrential rain poured over Zander's head as he knelt beside the wounded red fox. Early June in the oceanside town of Half Moon Bay meant plenty of spring rain. Situated on the west coast, smack dab between Canada and the United States, the Bay was technically an American town but many of her residents were Canadian.

He loved his hybrid Canadian American hometown. He was living the dream. He had his ideal veterinary practice and was minutes away from his mother if she needed anything. That was a mixed blessing. Seeing her regularly was great, but lately his mom and her friends had taken to setting him up with every single woman in town.

Today was another example of her desire to find him a wife. He was on his way home from the world's most awkward date with Mrs. Patterson's daughter, Julia. Lovely girl, but they had nothing in common. He wasn't surprised when she thanked him after their date and honestly told him she felt they hadn't clicked.

What he needed was a way to avoid dating. All these setups were taking too much time out of his already busy life. Never mind the money it cost to wine and dine an endless string of women. It wasn't in him to go on a date and not pay. Dutch was the best he could do and after eleven dates this month alone, he and his bank account were starting to dread another one.

He turned his attention back to the animal alongside the road. The fox's belly was swollen with pregnancy. Her hind leg was bent at an unusual angle, with the bone visible through a tear in her hide. The coppery tang of blood hit his nose and tastebuds. She'd bled a lot. Probably more than he could tell in this downpour.

Cars roared past, their headlights providing flashes of illumination that almost made his examination harder. Consistent dim light was easier to work in than having his eyes adjust to random bright and dark.

She growled low in her throat but didn't snap at him as he reached toward her. He was risking a bite and potentially rabies if she nipped him, but it didn't matter. He couldn't leave her here to die alongside the road.

"Hey, girl. You look like you're in a bad way." He inched closer. "I'm Dr. Bellamie. Call me Zander, I'm a vet. I look after animals." He placed his hand on her side. Her heart raced and she growled again but didn't nip at him. He couldn't help smiling. Sometimes he swore animals knew his intentions. In veterinary school, he easily treated animals his fellow students couldn't get close to.

Even as a kid, he'd been able to catch injured wildlife without harm. His grandmother always said he had an affinity for animals, and that they knew they were safe with him. Her words sounded like

3

superstitious nonsense, but on days like today, he hoped she was right.

Dark was falling fast. He stood to return to his truck to prep a sedative from supplies he kept in the medical bag he carried everywhere. The fox whined and he told her it would be okay. "I'll get you off this busy road and to the clinic where I can fix that leg."

With his hand back on her side, he flipped the cap off the needle. The poor animal was so weak she didn't even flinch when he punctured her skin. "That's my girl," he crooned as he pressed the plunger. "It's going to be okay."

He sprinted to his truck and grabbed a low-sided cardboard box from his chrome storage bin. Careful not to jostle her more than necessary, he slid her into the box and placed it on the floor of the truck. He blasted the heat to warm her. Even unconscious, she shivered from the drenching she'd received. He didn't bother to change into the dry clothing he kept in the back. Getting her to the clinic to determine the extent of her injuries and whether or not he could save her, and her kits was priority one. It was late in the year for whelping. With luck she'd survive birthing on top of her trauma.

King, his black lab, who had been waiting on the passenger seat, leaned over the box and sniffed the fox.

"Leave her alone." Zander chided gently. King immediately lay down on the front seat without taking his eyes off the fox.

He loved healing animals. Other people's pets were his life, but this, standing strong in an emergency, was what fueled his blood. The fear of something going wrong, battling with the certainty that he could save an animal; the excitement and hope of alleviating an animal's suffering. It didn't matter if it were a dog or a cat, or even a horse. The harder the case, the more he loved it. He excelled in a crisis. Helping animals, and people, fed his soul. This was why he was a vet.

His phone connected to Bluetooth as soon as he started the engine. He pressed the dashboard screen and said, "Call Jenny's cell phone." The speaker repeated his words and in seconds her phone was ringing.

"What's up boss? I was just about to tuck the kids in."

"I'm headed to the clinic with an injured fox. Are you able to come in to assist?"

"Hang on." Muffled voices said she must have covered the mouthpiece. "Yup, Todd will handle the rugrats. I'll head over right way. I need the overtime" she teased.

"See you there."

He had to drive through town and travel another five miles to his clinic on the northern outskirts of Half Moon Bay. The drive took an eternity and yet passed in seconds as he planned his diagnosis and treatment. Little Red, as he'd mentally dubbed the fox, would be a rehab case. If she survived, she'd be housed behind the clinic in one of his specially made runs until she was healed and had whelped and weaned her kits.

His rehab center currently housed a coyote, a white tail deer, and a snowy owl.

He pulled into the yard. The clinic lights blazed. Jenny had arrived before him. Excellent, she'd have things prepped for the exam. She was a darned good assistant. He stepped out of the truck and waited for King to hop down behind him. A rusty Toyota careened into the parking lot and screeched to a halt halfway into a stall.

Before he could react, a tall slender blonde leapt out of the car, slamming the door behind her hard enough that the car rocked. His brother's chef raced toward him. She stumbled to a stop when she saw his dog.

"King, sit." The massive dog dropped to his backside behind him.

"Zander! Help! I don't know what to do." Her voice shook with panic. She jerked forward in her haste to reach him, nearly falling.

He grasped her arms and held her upright until she regained her balance. "Take a deep breath, Heather. Tell me what's wrong."

Rain pelted down in thick gray sheets, but her arms were warm under his hands. Her eyes darted to the car and back to his face. She was seriously freaked out. Heather Olsen was usually the epitome of calm rationality. She ran her kitchen with a strong, understanding hand, and never got upset.

He'd admired her looks from the day they met at the grand opening of his brother's small inn. Since then, they'd shared an occasional conversation, and his admiration turned to respect and attraction. Her self-control, her generosity, and her smile were enticing. She was always happy, yet if you looked deep enough, it seemed a façade to cover something not quite so perfect. Her mouth smiled, but the smile didn't reach her eyes. Today that smile was replaced by naked fear.

"Please, you have to get that, that animal out of my car." Her voice rose with near hysteria. She shivered under his light grip.

"Let me get this injured fox inside, and I'll come help you."

She twisted her hands together and shifted back and forth. "Thank you."

Thunder rolled across the sky and lightning flashed. A sharp crack sounded as the lightning hit the ground somewhere close. She jumped into his arms.

Her body brushed his. She fit his body like she was made for him. For all that they were drenched, having her this close felt like coming home.

"Oh!" she exclaimed. "I hate thunder." She faked a laugh and backed away leaving him filled with longing to hold her tight and comfort her.

"That was a close strike. Let's get inside." He turned her toward the door and rounded his truck to get the fox. Little Red's chest rose and fell with a regular rhythm that was reassuring. "Can you get the door for me?" He pulled out the box, shouldered his truck shut, and strode to the entry. "King, come."

She rushed ahead and yanked open the door. She stood way back as King raced in out of the rain. Zander hurried inside with Heather right on his heels. Despite the humidity in the air and the scent of spring rain, she smelled of lemon and vanilla. It wasn't strong, but it was definitely there. It reminded him of lemon sugar cookies. Delish.

"Please, wait here. I'll only be a minute." He headed for the back, his cowboy boots squishing with each step. It was a good thing they were durable because they frequently stepped in things they shouldn't. After this drenching, it would take days for them to dry out. "I'll get my tech to start some exams while I help you."

Though distracted by his concern for the fox, he couldn't help thinking about Heather. She was only about five inches shorter than he was. He usually liked a woman he could look right in the eye. Heather's blue eyes were intriguing. Her hair was slicked down her back, water ran down her cheeks. She stood straight and tall despite her obvious distress. A smile crossed his face. She looked like a drowned rat, yet still had grace and dignity. Beautiful. Breathtaking. He shoved down the need growing in his heart.

Chapter 2

Zander was as enticing today as he was the first time she'd seen him at the inn's grand opening. He'd darted here and there, seeming to lend a hand everywhere. He'd been around a lot since then. They hadn't had many conversations, but she knew he was dependable and very easy to talk to. That's why, in her somewhat panicked state, she turned to him for help.

The fact that Zander Bellamie was extremely handsome was irrelevant. Tall, with neatly trimmed dark-blonde facial hair and lean strong muscles, he was temptation incarnate. She loved a man with a beard. He walked through a swinging door and greeted someone named Jenny. Jealousy prickled along Heather's arms. Who was Jenny?

She rolled her eyes at her own foolishness. Jenny, whoever she was, was of no consequence, because Heather had no interest in the very handsome Dr. Zander Bellamie. Forcing her mind away from the man, she looked around.

The clinic was spotless. Nothing out of place. Tall racks of pet supplies, toys and food lined two walls. There was a seven-chair waiting area in front of the reception desk. Zander's enormous black dog sat on a rubber mat near the door.

Beside him was a bin of neatly folded towels probably meant to dry off damp pets. She seriously needed one of those towels.

"Hey, boy," she said softly. She was afraid of dogs, okay, anything with four legs, but those towels were tempting. "Stay, okay?" Her voice shook. Dang it. Why did she have to run into two animals in one day? The last year had been horrid. Wasn't she due for a change in luck?

The dog tipped his head and stared at her, his tongue hanging out. He looked, dare she even think it, friendly? She inched over and grabbed a towel and quickly backed away. The dog didn't move. He seemed well trained. His head bobbed up and down like he was laughing at her. She scowled.

Heather squeezed moisture from her hair. She was growing out a short bob. Now it was just past her shoulders, and she could put it up again. She loved an updo, but she'd cut it for her ex who preferred short hair.

"Stop thinking about him," she muttered. "He's gone from your life. His opinion doesn't matter. You've moved on." She hung the towel on a chair and looked around the room. She laughed at the comical pictures of puppies and kittens on the wall. Zander had created a welcoming space. Obviously, he cared about his clients as much as he cared about his family.

He was a genuinely nice guy. Dating material ... except that he was her boss's brother. Besides, she wasn't looking to date after her last disastrous relationship. But if she was, she wouldn't look towards her employer's family. Not even if they were as attractive and compelling as Zander.

Zander stepped back into the waiting room and smiled. "There, Little Red's getting some x-rays and I can help you."

"Little Red?"

"The fox." He chuckled. "I name all my rescues." His phone chimed and he pulled it out and looked at the screen. He frowned and stuffed it back in his pocket. "Okay, Heather," he said, "tell me about this animal."

She felt a little silly now that she was away from the immediate danger of her unwanted passenger. She winced knowing she was pulling him from his patient. "Um. There's an animal in my car and I don't know what to do. I came here because you know animals, right?" She locked her knees to keep her legs from trembling as her fear resurfaced.

"Animal control might have been a better option, but you're here now, and I am good with animals. What kind of critter is it?" he asked as he headed to the front door.

She hurried behind him but didn't answer. This is the part she hated. Admitting her fears.

"Well?" He stopped by the door and looked at her, his brown eyes assessing.

"It's a huge cat of some kind." She stared down at the floor.

"There's a lynx in your car?" He blinked twice. "You drove here with a lynx in your car?"

"Not exactly." Heat flooded her face. She wanted to crawl into a hole and vanish.

"Look, Heather. I'm sorry to rush you, but I need to be in surgery, and I can't do that unless we solve your problem first. What's in your car?"

She stared at the floor again trying to find words to explain her predicament.

"Heather," he snapped. She heard him inhale and let the breath out slowly. "Look, you're obviously afraid and embarrassed. I understand that. Help me out here, okay?"

She glanced up, his eyes were kind, but the muscles in his jaw jumped.

"It's a cat. A feral cat. I think. It's huge. Biggest cat I ever saw." She shuddered. "It jumped in when I opened my door at the grocery store. I tried and tried but it wouldn't come out." She dashed away a stupid tear. "It growled at me. Nobody was around to help so I came here."

"Wait. What?" He frowned in disbelief. "I'm delaying surgery because a cat growled at you?" He shook his head. "Jeepers."

He turned away.

"Aren't you going to help me?" she called after him. *Was he abandoning her?*

"I need a cage, and gloves. Be right back." He muttered something under his breath, but she couldn't quite catch the words.

He came back and tossed a sweatshirt at her. "Put this on, before you freeze to death."

Two minutes later, they stood in the mist wearing matching hoodies bearing his clinic logo. Thankfully, the rain had tapered off. He opened the passenger door and leaned in. His shirt rode up revealing the most delectable backside she'd seen in ages.

You're not interested, Heather. Stop staring.

She heard a meow, then some murmuring from Zander. Slowly he backed out of the car, pulling the cage behind him.

"Is this your wild animal?" he asked, a hint of amusement in his voice. "It's a house cat. It's not feral and it didn't even object to the cage. You might have overreacted." He grinned.

He wasn't outright laughing at her, though he was entertained, but at least he had taken care of the pest for her. She stiffened her spine. "I had an extremely bad experience as a child." She couldn't stop a shudder of remembered fear. "I was attacked by a feral cat and badly injured. It's silly, but I can't get past it. Cats scare me spitless." She looked him in the eye, daring him to mock her further.

"I'm sorry to hear that. Sometimes fear is irrational." There was a comfort in his voice that she hadn't gotten from her father after she hid the scratches until they festered enough to put her in the hospital.

She looked up at him. His wet hair shone in the bright light over the clinic door. She wanted to slick it back off his forehead. She cleared a lump of something she didn't want to admit from her throat. "Sorry to take you away from your fox. What do I owe you?"

"Nothing. It's good. I'll put Fluffy here inside and start looking for his owner. Sorry I have to rush away. You have a lovely night." Cage in hand, he turned and walked away.

"Thank you," she yelled.

He waved over his shoulder as he hurried back inside, leaving her standing in the damp air wearing his hoodie and thinking about his backside. She wanted to be annoyed that he was amused by her fear, but he'd been kind enough to help her out and she appreciated it. Besides, it was easy to see why her fear might appear funny to someone who clearly excelled in handling animals.

He had been amused, but he'd helped without complaint, despite being busy. Zander Bellamie was one of the good guys. He was what her grandmother would have called a "heart guy." A man you could lose your heart to without even noticing. Not that she liked him.

Chapter 3

Heather was almost home when she realized she was still wearing his hoodie. Dang. She'd have to return it later. She was not going to bother him right now. He was busy and she was tired, no, exhausted, and she was still freezing. Why had the heavens opened up just as that crazy cat jumped into her car? Her childhood fear had frozen her in place, and she'd been drenched. Something prompted her to get into the car and go for help. Why going back into the store didn't occur to her was baffling.

She pulled behind the white brick apartment building she lived in and parked in her assigned stall. Groceries in hand, she headed upstairs to the suite she shared with her roommate, Quinn.

She let herself into the apartment and called out, "Quinn, I'm home. I've had one heck of a day." She heard giggling through Quinn's door and groaned. She was *entertaining* again. Quinn was a great roommate, but her boyfriend was a jerk. In the weeks since

Heather had moved in the pair had done nothing but fight.

"Don't let it bug you. Eventually, you'll be able to afford a place of your own." She put the groceries away, put the kettle on, and went to change into dry clothing. She sifted through her meager clothing and pulled out a pair of yoga pants. They fit well enough, but sure weren't top end. She'd lost all her designer duds when her ex had stolen her inheritance and trashed her reputation.

Heartbroken, she'd fled Toronto for lower mainland British Columbia, and had been rooming with a friend. Luck and that good friend had gotten her a one time catering job at Zander's brother's inn. She'd knocked that gig out of the park and had talked her way into a steady job.

Living in Half Moon Bay was something of an adjustment. Small town life had everything she needed, but she missed the anonymity of the city. She didn't know how Quinn managed to date such a jerk without thinking about so many eyes watching her every move. Privacy was nonexistent here.

"It doesn't matter," she muttered as she pulled on her pants and a clean T-shirt. Still chilled from her earlier dousing, she pulled Zander's hoodie back on. It was nearly dry and still warm from her body. Socks in hand she headed for the kitchen and brewed a pot of her special blend orange-mint tea. Someday, she'd sell her tea and sweets in her own shop. She had to stabilize her life, save her money, and buy a place with a garden for growing the herbs. That meant keeping her eye on the ball and not losing her job. That in turn meant staying away from Zander, despite her instant and continued attraction to him.

Funny, Zander and his three brothers looked a lot alike, but the only one that sparked even a glimmer of interest was Zander. She shrugged off the thought. The world worked in mysterious ways and since she wasn't interested in dating, Zander's attractiveness was of no consequence.

Quinn's door opened and Heather heard her talking by the front door. "Thanks. I needed that," Quinn's sultry whisper drifted into the kitchen.

"You bet, babe." Something about the way he said babe was dismissive and demeaning. Heather's hackles rose and she banked down the urge to ask Quinn what she saw in the arrogant man.

"What's up, Heather?" Quinn asked after she locked the door. "You look frazzled."

"Work was great, but a cat hopped in my car today and scared the ever-loving crap out of me." She shivered. "Cats terrify me." Her mind flashed back to being four, maybe five, when she tried to pick up a feral cat and it had raked its claws down her entire body. Afraid to tell her dad that she was playing with stray animals, she hadn't told him about the injury until she fell ill with a fever caused by the infected scratches. According to the doctor, she could have died from a blood infection.

Her skin prickled with remembered fear, and she almost felt the cat's claws gouging her stomach, thighs, and arms again. She shook off the feeling.

Quinn slouched into a chair and accepted the tea Heather offered her. "Thanks." Her straight black hair was caught up in a messy ponytail that hung halfway down her back. Her green eyes drooped with exhaustion.

"Oh, you must have been terrified. What did you do?" Quinn asked.

"I totally freaked out. I couldn't get it out of my car, so I drove to the vet office. It hissed and growled at me all the way there." She shuddered. "On top of that, it was pouring rain and I got drenched. The vet helped me get the cat out of the car and lent me a dry hoodie." She sat at the small wooden kitchen table and cradled her tea in her hands for warmth.

"Aren't all those Bellamies just about the hottest thing you've ever seen?" Quinn asked. "I considered asking Zander out. But he's too busy for me. He doesn't date much, not ever actually. He's always running around helping something or somebody."

"He's been around the inn a few times. He is cute, but I swear his phone is glued to his hand." She made an exasperated sound. "He got the cat out of my car and had the nerve to laugh at me. I mean not outright laugh, but he was amused." She frowned. He could have been more sensitive.

23

"You should make a play for him," Quinn said. "He's totally hot and you're sweet. You'd make a great couple. Maybe you could whip up some cookies for saving you from the cat. The way to a man's heart is through his stomach." She chuckled. "He sure wasn't interested in me nursing him back to health when he was bitten by a dog. Can you believe he said it's the only time he's ever been attacked by an animal? Animals just seem to like him. Not that I blame them. He's very likeable."

"He didn't have any trouble with that cat, that's for sure. But I have no interest in Zander Bellamie or any other man. Even if I did there's no possible way because he's my boss's brother and I am not going to mess up this job. Eventually I want to open my own shop. Nothing fancy, just a tea house and bakery." She'd told Quinn this more than once, but every time she said it aloud, it made the possibility more real.

"What about getting an investor, you know, a partner? Wouldn't that make it easier?" Quinn jumped up and grabbed a bag of Oreos from the cupboard. She paced the kitchen and nibbled a cookie.

"You know my history. I won't ever take a partner again. I need to do this on my own. No partners. No man. Just me." She banked down a sigh. She couldn't help but remember just how attractive and kind Zander was.

"Do you know what makes Zander laughing at me worse? My boss, Derrick, is having his whole family over for dinner tomorrow night and I'm cooking and serving. I won't be able to escape Zander. What if he mentions my issue with the cat? I'll be mortified. Plus, as much as the Bellamies hang out together all the time, they fight like cats and dogs. I do not want to become caught up in those crazy family dynamics."

Quinn laughed. "I've never seen a family that fights the way they do. It doesn't seem to matter though because if one of them needs something the rest of them are right there." She shook her head. "They fight like cats and dogs, but they're too good looking to be real."

"Clearly you've got a thing for the Bellamie brothers," Heather teased.

"Not really. I mean Tyson is hotter than Chris Hemsworth, but he's not for me. Tyson used to play football; I mean big-time football. He got taken out in a game. He busted up his knee and had to have it replaced. Now he's the principal of the high school. I don't think he looks at women at all, let alone someone like me."

"Don't sell yourself short. You're an amazing physiotherapist and a great person. Although I don't know why you're looking at Tyson when you're dating already."

"I don't want to talk about it. We should go out for dinner."

Quinn didn't seem to realize that if she was happy with her current man, she wouldn't be drooling over Tyson.

"I don't have the energy for that. How about I make something for us instead?" She'd love to eat out, but she had given herself a timeline. In three years, she would open her own shop. It might be here. It might be in the city. And the only way that was happening on schedule was if she saved every penny. She had already spent her discretionary funds for the month.

"Right, I keep forgetting about that. I should be a better roommate. How about if I pay for the ingredients and you cook? Then I won't feel guilty." She slid back into her chair and sipped her tea.

Heather straightened the small vase of flowers on the table. Roses and carnations. They appeared one day and though her roommate never mentioned them, she suspected she was supposed to believe that Quinn's man had sent them. Her roommate had a sad air of desperation about dating.

"Oh, letting you pay doesn't seem right. We'll split the cost of the food. I'll cook, and you do the dishes. How does that sound?" Doing dishes was her least favorite part of cooking.

"Good enough for me. What will we have? I feel like pork chops."

"Sounds perfect to me. I've got a fabulous new recipe I'm dying to try. I'll do baked cheesy potatoes, spiced applesauce, and chocolate lava cake for dessert." She was beat, but cooking was soothing and invigorating.

Morning came entirely too early for Heather. They'd stayed up way too late last night drinking wine and chatting. It had been years since she had a best friend, and Quinn was easy to talk to. They'd finally gone to bed at midnight, which wasn't particularly late, but she had to be up at five to get to work in time to make breakfast for the guests at the inn.

Five hours sleep was usually enough, but she'd been awake half the night having dreams about a certain veterinarian with a sweet smile and delectable backside. The best, and worst, part was that in her dreams, he returned her interest. Every time she started dreaming about him, she woke up. She'd been dreaming about him since her first glimpse of him at the inn's opening. It was starting to get out of hand. He was the chocolate bar hidden in the cupboard that you couldn't quite forget about.

No matter how many times she told herself she had no business being interested in him she still kept dreaming about Zander. Sometimes the dreams were hot, sometimes they were sweet and romantic. She didn't know which were more disturbing. She barely knew him. Zander Bellamie was a pain in her backside because her mind wouldn't stop thinking about him. She doubled down her resolve to keep her distance from him. No matter what.

She climbed out of bed and prepped for the day. While she was dressing, she went over the morning's menu and her plans for the family dinner in the evening. The Inn at Half Moon Bay had a breakfast buffet and served cookies all day. Derrick was considering opening for dinner service once the inn was more firmly established.

She was excited and nervous to cook her first full dinner at the inn. If she aced this meal, she'd be invited to expand the inn's service. Thinking about the night ahead, a giddy shiver raced down her spine. A succulent meal to open career opportunities and she was going to see Zander again.

She was in so much trouble.

Chapter 4

Zander drove to Bellamie High to pick up his baby brother Tyson on his way to the inn for dinner. The school was named after one of his ancestors who had done big things for Half Moon Bay. Ty spent too much time alone and sometimes had to be coerced into coming to dinner. Today he'd called and asked for a ride. Unusual.

He pulled into the principal's stall in the empty lot and shot Tyson a text. Five minutes later, Ty limped out of the school, locking the door behind him.

"Yo!" Tyson groaned as he climbed into the truck.

"What's with the limp?" Zander asked.

"Tough day today. I slipped on a wet spot in the hallway. Tweaked my knee a bit. It'll be fine by tomorrow." He massaged it for a second.

"It better be. Or I'll drag you to physio myself. When are you going to replace Harry Webb? The man can hardly stand. He's a terrible janitor."

"I was going to, but then his wife died. After that, I couldn't take away his work. It's all he has left. I asked the school board to hire an assistant for him. It's a lot of work for a healthy man, let alone a man in his late sixties. I figure we can slowly phase Harry out. Let him down easy." He buckled his seatbelt and rolled the window down a crack. Ever since his accident, his brother hated being cooped up.

"That's a good plan. You better carry it through," Zander chided. Tyson had never succumbed to the fame that surrounded his winning seasons. When he was knocked out of the game, he seemed to take it in stride. His brother was hiding behind a socially acceptable mask. He'd lost some of his natural optimism and his normally upbeat expression carried too many frowns these days.

Tyson was the total opposite to Derrick, a discharged military veteran with too many tattoos, a too loud motorbike, and a too big chip on his shoulder. The only one of Zander's brothers with his life together was Jacob, though even he was struggling. He had left a huge business empire in Seattle and had brought his thirteen-year-old daughter, Ella, home to Half Moon Bay, after his ex-wife died.

"Do we need to stop for anything?" Tyson asked, interrupting Zander's worries.

"Nope. I grabbed a couple bottles of wine to go with dinner. I brought flowers for Mom, Ella, and Lexi. Shouldn't need anything else." He backed out of the stall and headed for the street.

"Flowers for a thirteen-year-old girl? That seems excessive."

"Not at all. Ella's an important part of this family. I want her to know that. Maybe knowing how much we care will help her feel like she belongs here. She's really missing her old friends and it's hard on a kid when your mom dies. She probably feels abandoned."

"True. You think of everything." Exasperation filled Tyson's voice. "Typical Zander. Always watching out for everyone else."

He refused to be drawn into the argument. Tyson made no bones about how much he resented the fact the Zander didn't hide his concern for their family. When his father passed, Zander refused to let his mother bear the responsibility for the family alone. He was who he was and wasn't going to change just to lessen his brother's hurt feelings.

"Any dateable teachers this year?" he asked instead of continuing the fight Tyson was trying to start. He checked for oncoming cars before turning toward the inn.

"Not a one. Both new teachers are in their early twenties, entirely too young for me, not that I'd date my staff. Still, we were lucky to get them. Everyone wants to live in the city these days. Sometimes, I can't say I blame them. Do you know how hard it is to date in a place like this? I'll tell you. It's impossible. I'm the principal of the high school. I have a reputation to maintain. I can't date just anyone, and I can't be seen dating too often. I have a moral image to project." He pushed out a harsh breath. "Sometimes I miss being a jock and having women throwing themselves at me all the time."

Zander barked out a laugh. "Eight years in the big leagues and you dated three, maybe four women?

Even when you were buried in chicks you stuck to yourself."

"True enough. But at least I had options." Abruptly he turned the tables. "How about you? Any dates lined up?"

"When would I have time to date? I've got the clinic, the rescue animals, I'm doing Mom's yardwork. I've been helping out at the inn. I don't have the time or inclination to date."

He'd never admit it, he'd enjoyed teasing Heather yesterday. She'd been terrified of a house cat, but still spunky, despite her fear. He couldn't wait to see her again. In Half Moon Bay it was never long before you bumped into someone unless they were a total recluse.

"Maybe if you stopped trying to mother all of us, you'd have time to run your own life," Tyson complained.

"Maybe when you all start running your own lives instead of running from crisis to crisis, I won't have to babysit you," he snapped back. As much as the idea of not having to keep tabs on everyone pleased him, it saddened him too. They were a close family and worrying about each other was natural. He was just more open about it than his brothers were. They were firm believers in the bro-code … never ask another man about his life or problems.

A motorcycle roared by them traveling way faster than the speed limit. Derrick! Sometimes it seemed like his brother was bent on taking his own life. He'd been less wild while doing renovations on the inn for Jacob. But since Jacob's return, he'd slid backward into some of his bad habits. Zander sighed. At least Derrick appeared to be headed toward the inn and dinner and wasn't blowing the family off.

The inn rang with loud voices as Zander and Tyson stepped inside. Jacob and Derrick were fighting again. It was only weeks ago that Zander had straightened Jacob's nose after Derrick punched him in the face during an argument. Zander was a veterinarian, but when his mom called, he'd rushed to the inn to doctor his brother's busted up face.

"We're here," he called out, hoping to stop the bickering.

Ella rushed out of the other room to give him a hug, her pretty brown hair flying behind her. She leaned against his chest and sighed. "They fight all the time."

"They always have. We all do," he reassured her. "We're different than a lot of families, but when push comes to shove, we're here for each other. We'll do anything to protect each other, and more than that to protect you, munchkin."

"I know. But I still don't like it." Her face pinched into a worried frown.

"Here, I brought these for you." He handed over the bouquet of brightly colored daisies.

"Oh, thank you." She hopped up and kissed his cheek, a smile blossoming in her eyes.

"You're welcome. What's for dinner?" he asked, going for the distraction. Ella hadn't spent much time with the family before she'd moved back in with Jacob. She wasn't used to their rowdy way of doing things. Deep in his heart, he knew she'd adapt. She probably didn't even realize that she fought with her father the same way everyone else did.

37

"Chicken something. I don't know the proper name, I forgot to ask Heather. She's great. She even let me help cook. I can't decide if I'm going to be a painter, or a chef, when I grow up. Not that I'm not grown up already, even if Dad won't admit it."

"Munchkin, enjoy being a kid and keep on trying new things. You never know what your gift is until you stumble on it."

"You have a gift with animals. Grandma says so. Just like Dad has a gift for business." She grabbed him and Tyson by the elbows and dragged them through the inn, past the front desk and sitting room, toward the dining room. "Heather says we'll eat as soon as you're here. Good thing you weren't any later, dinner would have been ruined," she declared with all the drama of a teenager.

Laughing, he allowed himself to be towed to the table and took a seat between his mother and Jacob's girlfriend, Lexi. He leaned over and pressed a kiss to his mother's cheek and passed her a bouquet of carnations. He gave Lexi a pink and yellow bouquet of mixed flowers. Tyson set the wine on the table. "Hi,

Mom," Zander said. "You look great. Did you get your hair cut?"

She smiled. "Thank you, dear. The flowers are lovely. I did get my hair cut. Thanks for noticing."

He didn't see any difference in her hair, but he recalled her mentioning going to the salon.

"Zander, have you met Heather?" Jacob asked. "She catered for us when the caterer we hired couldn't make it. Turns out it was a good thing. She needed work and I needed a chef. She's more than that, the woman cooks like a five-star chef. I don't know what she's doing in a tiny place like Half Moon Bay when she could be cooking for a high-end restaurant."

"We've talked a time or two," he said when his brother stopped singing Heather's praises. Zander had mingled at the inn's opening, but it had been an absolute zoo with Jacob rolling in via helicopter at the last second. He had talked to Heather a few times, and now that he'd met her again, at the clinic, he was curious about her.

"Here she is now," his mom exclaimed. "Isn't she lovely, Zander?"

"Mom don't try and hook up my staff. They're off limits," Derrick growled.

Zander turned toward the door to the kitchen. Heather, his Heather, stood in the doorway in a pristine white chef's jacket. Whoa! "His Heather?" What was he thinking. He barely knew her.

Her blonde hair was pulled into a tight, no-nonsense bun. She had a huge tray of appetizers in her hands and a nervous look on her face. She glanced around the room but didn't seem to meet anyone's eye.

"Heather. Nice to see you again," he said, unable to stop grinning. Something about her made him smile.

"Dr. Bellamie. I didn't expect to see you here." she lied. He could tell when she avoided his eyes. She cooked for a Bellamie. How could she not expect to see him at a Bellamie family dinner? And what was with her calling him doctor?

"Call me Zander, please."

"Oh," Lexi said. "I didn't realize you knew each other. Do you have a pet, Heather?" Lexi was the friendliest person Zander knew. She chatted to everyone and had a gift for putting them at ease. She would be the consummate innkeeper's wife once they married.

"No pets," Heather said. "I bumped into Zander yesterday."

"I rescued her from a wild animal." He chuckled.

"That sounds exciting." Ella clapped her hands. "Tell us about it."

Heather started placing the delicate appetizers in front of everyone. "Tonight, we have two appetizers. Baked cranberry brie bites and mushroom pastries with a tomato garlic aioli sauce."

"But what about the wild animal?" Ella bounced on her chair.

"There's nothing to tell," Heather moved around the table carefully setting each duo of appetizers before one of his family members.

"Of course, there's something to tell," Zander said. "I had just gotten back to the clinic after picking up a fox on the side of the road. Poor thing had a broken leg. I was going inside when this car screeched up at a hundred miles an hour and a screaming woman got out." He gestured toward Heather who frowned back.

"I wasn't screaming." She wanted to beg him to shut up. Mortification stole her voice.

"You were." He winked at her. "Anyway. She was freaking out because there was a wild animal in her car." He shrugged. "What's a guy to do? I captured the wild beast and saved the damsel in distress."

"What was it?" Ella asked, her eyes wide with excitement only a young teen could generate.

"A cat. A domestic feline. Totally tame." Zander's laugh brought heat to her cheeks. How could he do this to her? She wanted to fling herself out of the window, hit the ground, and run until she was a million miles away.

Heather set a plate in front of his mother. She reached across him with his plate, and in a fit of pique, tipped it so the mushroom pastry dropped onto his lap. "Oops. Sorry. Let me get a cloth for that." She grabbed her empty tray and hurried to the kitchen. *That'll teach him.*

Behind her he said, "You guys eat. I'll be back in a second."

"You did that on purpose," he accused once the door between the kitchen and dining room was shut. He strode toward her.

She backed up until she bumped into the sink.

"You can't prove that." She crossed her arms.

"I don't have to, you just confessed." His laughing eyes mocked her embarrassment. "Why did you dump that on me?"

"What?" she squeaked. "Because you're a total jerk. You told everyone I'm afraid of cats and made me sound like an idiot. Why couldn't you keep your mouth shut?"

"What was I supposed to tell them?" He stepped toward her. They were almost toe-to-toe. Her light scent tickled his nose even over the delicious smells of dinner.

"Nothing. You could have said nothing. You didn't have to embarrass me." She leaned away from him.

The accusation hit home. *He'd been a jerk.* Regret scraped across his conscience. "You're right." Gosh, she was beautiful. Irresistible. "I'm sorry." Unbidden, his hand lifted, and his finger traced a line down her cheek in front of her ear. He'd wanted to touch her from that first moment in the rain. No, since the first time he saw her. Her skin was rose-petal soft under his fingertip. "I am so, so sorry," he whispered.

"It's okay," her voice trembled.

"No, it isn't. Sorry," he said again. He leaned forward and brushed his lips across hers. He hadn't meant to kiss her at all. He'd only come to the kitchen to apologize.

Once their lips touched, he was lost. Reality spiraled away until nothing remained except Heather and bliss. He pressed forward, she pressed back. Her lips hard at first, then softening under his as she gave in to the caress between them.

He pushed for more, to learn her needs, when she abruptly slapped his face.

"What the hell are you doing?" Her mouth snapped shut and her teeth ground together audibly.

44

"Kissing you?" He quirked up an eyebrow and moved back half a step. "You returned the kiss." His cheek stung like the devil.

"I did not." She pushed him away and scurried to the other side of the kitchen.

"Did too." He followed her.

"Did not." He edged closer as she backed up. Her gaze kept darting away and back again. Like she wanted to look at him but couldn't quite manage it. Was his interest mutual? She looked intrigued, not afraid. A sweet half smile played on her lips.

"Okay, maybe I did kiss back. But it isn't going to happen again. You have no right. You'll get me fired."

Was that her objection? "I've got some clout with your boss; you won't get fired," he joked to ease the tension.

She frowned. "Not funny. You had no right to kiss me, Dr. Bellamie. None at all. I didn't want it."

He took two steps backward and hung his head. "I asked you to call me Zander. You're right. I apologize. I should have asked permission first. I don't know why I kissed you. It won't happen again." *God, he was a*

45

first-class jerk. What was he thinking? Kissing her without warning? It didn't matter that for a second, she'd kissed him back. He'd overstepped.

The kitchen door swung open and Derrick came in. He took one look at Zander's face and stormed over to them. "What's going on here?"

"Just getting to know your chef." Zander smirked.

Heather elbowed him in the stomach.

Zander doubled over in pain and surprise. Heather's muffled snort of laughter took some of the sting from his aching stomach. He held up his hands in surrender. "I'll just go clean up elsewhere." He hobbled, hunched over, toward the small bathroom off the kitchen. "I apologize, Heather. It won't happen again."

"It better not. Leave my staff alone, or I'll use your castration bander on you." Derrick barked.

It was an idle threat, but it made Derrick's point. He'd crossed a line he shouldn't have. But dang, Heather was a sweet temptation that was hard to resist. As he closed the bathroom door, Zander heard his brother apologizing. "Sorry for that, Heather. My brothers are all animals. Every single one of them. If he bothers you again, let me know. I won't tolerate abuse of my staff, from anyone."

"He didn't mean any harm."

She was one tough woman. Strong too. He rubbed his aching belly and ignored the tingling in his lips. That two second kiss was going to linger in his mind for a while.

Chapter 5

Heather's gaze flipped back and forth between her boss and the closed bathroom door. What had Zander been thinking? He'd kissed her. At work. She didn't even know him. Her lips still tingled from the brief caress. She'd reacted without meaning too, both to the kiss and in slapping him. Zander Bellamie made her feel off-kilter and his kiss left her legs feeling like overcooked noodles.

"I'm sorry," she said to Derrick. He'd probably fire her now. He wasn't known for his patience. He was known for his tattoos and wicked big motorbike. She had her doubts about him at first, but he was a good manager.

"It's not your fault. That's just my brother messing with my life. I'll talk to him. It won't happen again. Are you hurt?" His shoulders were tense, and his voice tight. His arms flexed making his tattoos ripple dangerously. For the life of her, she couldn't decide if he was upset with her or his brother.

If that kiss gets me fired .... It was a great kiss but not worth losing her job for.

Water ran in the bathroom as Zander cleaned up. The sauce would probably stain his jeans. She should offer to replace them. She'd been foolish to spill on him to get back at him for revealing her fear. Her emotions spiraled out of control with astonishing speed.

Something about him made her act irrationally. First with her embarrassment, then with that flood of sweet sensation sweeping over her when they kissed. She'd struck out in shock, not pique or anger. She enjoyed those few intimate seconds.

No! She didn't want to be attracted to a man. She wasn't foolish enough to be taken in by a handsome face again. She'd taken that ride. Never again. Her gullibility had nearly ruined her career, and this was her chance to build fresh. There was no way on earth she'd put that at risk, not even for someone as handsome as Zander Bellamie. Because for all that he laughed and teased her, there was something indefinable about him that tugged at her heart.

Wrong time. Wrong place. Wrong man.

"It's fine, Derrick. I think he was mad that I spilled on him because I was embarrassed that he told everyone I'm afraid of cats."

Her boss shook his head. "What normal person kisses someone they're angry with? Idiot brothers." He took a cross-armed stance between her and the bathroom door. "I'll just wait here until he goes back to the table. Go ahead and do what you need to do." His voice was serious, but kind.

"Your appetizer will get cold. You should go and enjoy it. I'm fine. Really." She grabbed him by the arm and led him toward the dining room. "I promise I'll let you know if he gets out of hand again."

He gave her an obstinate look but allowed himself to be pushed from the room. She picked up a knife to slice the crispy coated chicken breasts before plating dinner but kept one eye on the bathroom door. She wasn't afraid of Zander; she just didn't want to allow him the chance to startle her again. He was much too attractive, and his kiss was too potent.

"No men," she whispered under her breath just as the door opened.

"Pardon me?" he asked politely from across the kitchen.

"Nothing. Just talking to the chicken." Heat flooded her face. What an airhead response! She was losing her mind. Zander Bellamie had a way of throwing her off her game without even trying.

"O-kay," he drew the word into two questioning syllables. "Again, I apologize."

"Apology accepted. Please, go eat." *Would he just go away already?*

"It's just that ..." He looked chagrined. "I've been thinking about you since yesterday."

She set down the knife, intending to ask him why that made it okay to kiss her. Something else entirely flew from her mouth. "I thought about you too."

"You did?" His expression morphed to glee before her eyes.

"Sorry, Dr. Bellamie, I'm not interested in you. Or your delicious kisses." She snapped her mouth shut, then opened it long enough to say, "Go eat. This discussion is over. And I'd appreciate it if you didn't tell anyone else about my phobia."

"Delicious? Okay, I'll give you that, and again, please call me Zander." He stared at her for several interminable moments. His head tipped left, then right. Finally, he nodded.

His phone chimed and he pulled it out and texted something. He waited for a response without lifting his eyes from the screen. After fifteen seconds it beeped, and his fingers worked their magic again. For the next three minutes, it was as if she didn't exist. His entire being was focused on the device in his hand. Finally, he slid it into his pocket.

He looked up at her and smiled enigmatically. "We're all good then?"

"We're good."

He sauntered out of the kitchen leaving her certain the battle between them was far from over. She sagged against the counter with a heavy sigh. How could all this upheaval start because she was afraid of cats?

"Oh my gosh! I slapped my boss's brother!" She was incredibly lucky Derrick hadn't misunderstood and fired her. When Zander came out of the bathroom, the handprint on his face was still bright red. There was no way his family was going to miss it. She had better start looking for a new job.

Wait. Derrick hadn't fired her!

Yet.

She could still wow him with dinner. She doubled her speed and cut the rest of the chicken. She put it under a cover and went to clear the appetizer plates. The family was bickering good-naturedly when she entered the dining room. Derrick and Zander kept the conversation going while she picked up the dishes. She appreciated that they weren't letting anyone mention the mark on Zander's face, though his mother gave Heather a knowing look.

"Heather, can I help serve?" Ella asked. "Please."

The question surprised her. "Well, you did help cook, so if it's okay with your father, I don't mind."

"Go ahead." Jacob seemed happy that Ella was interested. Heather had overheard more than one conversation which revealed he was having trouble raising a teen alone. Lexi's addition to their small

54

family was helping them forge a better relationship, but at times they still struggled.

Ella followed her back to the kitchen. "This is what we need to do." She explained the process, and Ella helped her finish plating the food.

"Did you slap my uncle?" she blurted, sounding awed.

"He behaved inappropriately. I slapped him for it." She paused, not sure how to make a youth understand. "Violence is never the answer, but I won't let a man kiss me without asking. I need to apologize for striking him. He shouldn't have kissed me. I shouldn't have slapped him. We both messed up." She slammed her mouth shut before she muddled the situation even more.

"He kissed you! He must really like you," Ella blurted. "Daddy says he doesn't date anyone. Ever. It's because he's too wrapped up in other people's lives and pets," she added, clearly parroting her father. "I think Gramma tries to get him to go on dates, but he doesn't want to. Maybe that's why he kissed you."

55

The convoluted logic escaped her, so Heather changed topics. "Okay, grab two plates and follow me. We serve from the right side. You start with your grandma, then Lexi and your dad. I'll start on the other side of the table, and we'll work our way around." Ella understood the discussion was over and eagerly carried the plates out.

"Tonight's dinner is crispy chicken served with a white wine mushroom sauce, a medley of fresh seasonal vegetables from the farmer's market, and lemon herbed rice." She set the first plate in front of Derrick.

She took both serving trays into the kitchen, fretting about the meal, the kiss, and mostly about the slap. She refused to allow herself to think about how she wasn't nearly as upset about the kiss as she should be.

"What's wrong with you?" she muttered under her breath as she prepped the individual strawberry shortcakes for dessert. "The last man you dated ruined your life. Dating the boss's brother is a recipe for disaster. It doesn't matter that he's handsome or that his kiss scalded you down to your toes."

Ruthlessly, she shoved the thoughts aside and went to clear dinner plates. This meal was a test. If it went well and they opened for dinner service, there would be staff to serve and clear, and she'd be free to follow her passion to cook and manage the kitchen. She nearly giggled in excitement as she entered the dining room.

"That was amazing," Lexi declared.

"It sure was," Mrs. Bellamie said. She'd met the middle-aged woman at the open house, but for the life of her could not remember her first name. "The vegetable medley was the perfect accompaniment for the chicken and rice. You're a talented cook. You'll make someone a fabulous wife."

"Thank you. I'm glad you enjoyed it." She wasn't used to dealing directly with diners, so she ignored the fabulous wife comment and cleared the dishes in silence. She was arranging the smaller desert dishes on a tray when Ella skittered into the kitchen.

"Dad says I can help serve dessert, if you don't mind." She twisted her hands together and bounced on her toes though she was obviously trying to stay still.

"I don't see why not. Do you like working in the kitchen?"

"I like cooking, but Dad doesn't usually let me. Lexi lets me help sometimes. I like art too. Lexi lets me use her paints." The teen shrugged with a seeming lack of concern, but Heather knew these small things were more important than she let on.

"Perhaps, over the summer, I can teach you a few things in the kitchen. Let me discuss it with your father. No guarantees, but I'll come up with a plan and see if he goes for it."

"Okay." Again, fake nonchalance hid the excitement in Ella's eyes.

"My grandmother taught me to cook. What started as a fun way to spend time with her turned into a career." She was happy to share her skills with Ella.

"Shall we serve?" They picked up their trays. "Same plan as before. Remember to keep the tray balanced as you remove plates. Don't take them all from the same side or it will tip. Watch the berry juice and topping doesn't drip on anyone."

"Like you did with Uncle Zander?"

"Exactly! Slow and careful is always best."

She glanced at Zander as she served his family. Every time she looked his way, he was looking at her. The third time he winked, she nearly lost her grip on the plate she held. Spilling twice in one night could be a career ending move. She forced herself to ignore Zander because the only person she needed to impress was her boss.

She concentrated on the task at hand, though her hands trembled knowing Zander was watching her. Leaving the dining room, she stole one last glance and noticed his phone in his hand. Couldn't he leave the thing alone long enough to share a meal with his family?

She was scrubbing the roasting pans when Jacob came into the kitchen.

"Heather, come into my office, so we can talk. Please." Whatever Jacob had to say must be important because he owned the inn and Derrick was the day-to-day manager.

Slowly, hiding her nerves, she dried her hands and hung her apron on a hook. She used the apron for dishes, to reduce the mess on her chef jacket. She followed him to his small office and stood in the doorway.

"Please, come in. Sit." He waved toward a chair and took a seat behind his desk. His face was totally expressionless.

She perched on the chair edge and clenched her hands in her lap. This was where she got fired. She could see it in his eyes. She bit the inside of her lip to keep from begging for her job.

"I saw Zander's face. Is knowing my brother will be around the inn frequently going to be a problem for you?" His tone was as flat as his expression, and she had no idea where he was going with this. Was this a warning, or something else?

She took a moment to consider the question. "No, I don't believe so. I'm certain he won't be in the kitchen often and if he is, I think I can trust him not to repeat what happened tonight. I apologize for spilling on him. I hope that aside from the spill, dinner was acceptable." Hoped, nothing! She was praying for all she was worth. Mentally, she had her fingers, toes, legs, and arms crossed for good luck.

"Dinner was excellent. Can you write up a proposal for expanding the inn's food service? Include a prospective menu. Give it to Derrick by Monday, please. We'd like to expand in time for the July long weekend. We're booked solid for the event, and it would be a great time to unveil our new service."

It appeared that the subject of Zander's transgression was forgotten. She did a mental happy dance but stayed still in her seat. "I can do that." She paused. "Can I ask a question?"

"Go ahead. I'm always open to questions from my employees."

"Ella said she'd like to learn more about cooking. I was wondering if you would mind if I had her assist with some meal preparations, and maybe gave her a few lessons." She was eager to teach Ella. Sharing her love of cooking would fill her heart with joy.

61

Jacob frowned. "I suppose that will be okay if it doesn't interfere with homework. And please don't let her get in your way. Same with Zander. Don't let him bother you. If he becomes a pest, let me know immediately."

"I'll do that. Ella won't be a problem. She loves the kitchen. She's got good basic skills. Someone taught her very well."

"I don't cook much, and probably don't let her help often enough. I guess that was her mother's doing."

"A job well done." Hopefully, he knew she meant the praise and wasn't just sucking up to her boss.

"Thanks. Get that proposal to Derrick. We'll look it over and call you to discuss details." He stood, indicating the brief discussion was over.

Back in the kitchen, she did a happy dance and hugged herself. She got to expand meal service. She couldn't wait to share her news with Quinn. This was the first step in rebuilding her career, her reputation, and her life. Finally, after months of hoping for change, and striving to achieve it, things were looking up.

She'd barely donned her apron again when the kitchen door swung open. If people kept coming in, she'd never finish dishes. She pretended she didn't hear the door and busied herself scrubbing a bit of baked on chicken skin.

"I hear you're going to be expanding your role here. Congratulations," Zander said from across the room. She closed her eyes. She did not want to talk to him. Just the sound of his voice had her lips remembering the pressure of his.

"Thank you." She didn't look at him. She rinsed the dish and set it onto the draining board. *Please go away. Please go away.* She inspected the second roaster and started scrubbing.

"I can cook, but I'm not great at it," he said. "Maybe I'll come around more if meals like tonight will be my reward."

He was trying to get a reaction and she refused to be baited. "I'm sure your brother will welcome the added income."

His laughter burst through the quiet kitchen. Deep and husky, it scraped against her nerves. Gooseflesh rose on her arms. *You do not like his laugh.* Footsteps came closer and he leaned his backside on the counter beside her. He was close enough to touch and she fisted her hands in the water to keep from reaching out.

"Derrick won't charge me to eat. I'm family."

"I'd charge you," she quipped back. Even in the kitchen with the lingering smells of roasted chicken dinner, she caught the slightest whiff of his unique scent. Clean and soapy, like he'd just stepped out of the shower. She closed her eyes and savored it. She hadn't noticed how he smelled yesterday at the clinic. Drenched from the rain, all she had smelled was wetness. Today, after that kiss and with him beside her it was a pleasant distraction.

"I guess we'll let Derrick decide." He gave her a little elbow bump.

She nodded. It wasn't up to her who paid for their meals. She was the chef and kitchen manager, nothing more. Pride surged through her. She was making her way back up.

"Your family seems nice. I talked to your mom a bit at the opening. She's sweet."

"Ha." His laugh was wry. "Mom's got a backbone of steel if you cross her." His grin turned soft and loving. "She's a great person, except for trying to get me married off all the time. Other than that, I don't know how she puts up with the four of us.

"Yeah, I heard about the argument between Derrick and Jacob the day the inn opened. It sounds like it was something else." She scrubbed a particularly stubborn spot to keep from turning to gaze at him. "Tell me about them."

"You've got to watch out for my brothers. Jacob's a workaholic. Tyson's got issues over his aborted football career. Being a high school principal wasn't on his to do list. Derrick ... well he's just Derrick. Mad at the world and itching for a fight."

"And Zander? What's his issue?" She couldn't resist teasing him.

"Zander's amazing in all respects," he quipped. "No issues at all. He's a talented veterinarian. His mother's favorite son. Kind to strangers. Rescues fair maidens from wild creatures."

She risked a glance at him at the last comment. His wink went straight to her heart. He was an irrepressible flirt. Just like her ex. Any attraction she might have been feeling, vanished at the comparison.

"And humble too, I see."

"It isn't vain if it's true," he countered.

It felt like he was aiming for something with all the self-praise, but she couldn't put her finger on where he was headed. "Time will tell if Zander is all that and a bag of chips, or just a big old blowhard with an ego the size of Ontario."

"I think you mean the size of Texas. We are in the United States."

"Well, I'm from Canada and if the province fits ...." She rinsed the roaster and started loading the pots into the industrial dishwasher for sterilization. The dishwasher was one of the first changes she'd made when Jacob hired her. You couldn't have food service without proper equipment.

"The US is far superior to Canada, you crazy Canuck."

"In your dreams, Yankee Boy, in your dreams."

They stared at each other, and she couldn't help but laugh. He frowned for a second before joining in. "Honestly," she said, trying to catch her breath, "we live in two amazing countries."

They high fived and she marveled at how well they seemed to click. Not that it mattered, because she wasn't interested in her boss's brother. Even as her brain told her she wasn't interested, her heart whispered that she might be. She was attracted and she barely knew him ... a fact that didn't bode well for her heart. How in the world was she going to keep her distance?

Chapter 6

Stars popped out of the night sky as Zander sat in his truck outside the inn. Stargazing was a regular part of his life. There was something peaceful and invigorating about watching the night sky come to life right in front of him. He could name dozens of constellations. As always, he was struck by Cassiopeia, the queen. It was one of his favorites because of its ease of recognition. The erratic W-shape was easy to spot. It was the first his father ever taught him. Tonight, for some reason, it reminded him of his brother's chef.

Heather Olsen was a distraction he didn't need. He had a mother and brothers to worry about. There were animals to care for, and a business to run. Unfortunately, there was something about Heather that turned him into an absolute flirt. Sure. He flirted with every woman in town. It was a defense mechanism of sorts. Women stayed away because he flirted too much. But flirting with Heather felt different, like there was something at stake. The sensation was unnerving. He shrugged off the thought as he drove home from the family dinner.

Though the evening was drawing to a close, he rolled slowly through town taking in the sights. Main Street with its quaintly named stores always made him smile. The Barnacle Bookshop, the Buried Treasures antique store, and the Old Bay Bait and Tackle Shop, which was right next to the Tide's In Café, and one of his favorite shops was Not Washed Up Yet, a secondhand consignment shop for clothing. It was the nature of his job that he destroyed a lot of clothing, despite wearing coveralls and lab coats. It made sense to buy used clothing for work. There was a light on inside the shop, and he saw Ellery sorting donations.

He was tempted to stop and talk with her, to catch up. But they'd dated a few times and despite it ending amicably, he worried that she'd take a surprise visit the wrong way. She was a lovely woman but didn't spark any romantic interest in his heart. Not like Heather.

Seeing her there, all alone, made his mind roll forward to a wife and family of his own. Someday, when his business was under control, when his brothers had their lives together, he'd have time for dating and marriage. Even once he married, he'd save room for his family's needs.

As he drove past, the tower clock on the town hall warned him it was later than he thought. How had it gotten so late? The evening had flown by. He had thoroughly enjoyed himself, not just because he kissed Heather, though that was a factor, as was the anticipation of catching glimpses of her as she served dinner.

He should be exhausted but he felt like he'd consumed too much coffee. He was wired, in a good way. Like he couldn't wait for whatever came next. He shook his head. He wasn't a kid to be excited over nothing. What was his mind trying to tell him?

His phone vibrated in his pocket, and he pulled into the library lot and parked to answer it.

"Dr. Bellamie," he greeted the caller.

Mrs. Miggins' frightened voice burst over the line. "Dr. B. Help me. Peachie-Pie is sick. Really sick. I don't know what's wrong." The septuagenarian was a lonely woman who doted too much on her pet. She'd managed to bypass his answering service and found his cell phone number.

"Can you bring Peaches to the clinic? I'm only five minutes away."

"Yes. Thank you." He could barely make out the words over her tears.

She was at the clinic when he arrived, she must have called him while driving. Not good. Mrs. Miggins still had all her faculties, and was a decent driver, but when distraught, nobody needed to be on the phone while driving.

The second he parked, she jumped out of her aging yellow Cadillac, the dog in her arms.

"Dr. Bellamie. Bless you for coming. Thank you. Please help her."

Even from eight feet away, the dog's raspy breathing was audible. He knew in an instant that

Peaches had swallowed something she shouldn't have been eating.

He opened the door and held it open for Mrs. Miggins. He flipped the lock behind her and led her to an exam room.

"What was the last thing Peaches did, before her breathing changed?"

The frightened woman stared down at the floor and refused to meet his eye.

Carefully, he listened to the Chihuahua's breathing and repeated gagging. Whatever was lodged in his/her throat was a problem, but the dog didn't seem to be in immediate danger unless it started to panic.

"Mrs. Miggins, I cannot help her, unless I know what happened. You don't want Peaches to die, do you?" The words were harsh, but they'd been down this road more than once. She flat out refused to stick to kibble. He cradled the dog in one arm and used his fingers to pry her mouth open. He peered down her throat.

"Is that a bone?" Surely, she wasn't that foolish.

"Maybe." Her voice trembled.

"What kind of bone and how did she get it?" He'd warned her a dozen times not to give bones to the miniscule dog.

"She jumped up and stole it off my plate while I was in the washroom."

"Mrs. Miggins," Zander said, aiming for patience. "You know as well as I do, that Peaches can barely climb stairs. There is no way she could jump onto a chair and get up on the dining table to steal a bone."

She wept in earnest now. "I know," she whispered. "But she was just so hungry and so cute I couldn't resist."

His phone started vibrating in his pocket. He ignored it. "I'm hoping I don't have to sedate her to get the bone out. You'll have to hold her still." He set the distressed pooch on the exam table.

Mrs. M's hands trembled, and tears streamed down her cheeks, but she managed to hold the dog in place. Pulling the bone was more traumatic for Mrs. Miggins than it was for Peaches. Zander freed the bone and examined it.

"A chicken bone? Those are the worst. How many pieces did she get?"

"Just one. I swear." She clutched her hands in front of her chest as if praying.

"If you must feed her treats, get proper treats here, or from the pet store. Maybe you could find a recipe and bake your own. Just, please, stop feeding her table scraps." He felt terrible for both the dog and its owner. "I understand that she's your baby. Pets are great for our hearts. They are family. But if you don't stop feeding her human food, she won't last until the end of the year."

"I promise."

He suspected it was another in a long line of false promises. "I'm going to keep Peaches overnight for some tests and for observation." The dog was fine. After repeated lectures on feeding, worry was the only thing that might penetrate Mrs. M's stubborn attitude. "I'm hoping she'll be fine in the morning."

"But I haven't slept alone since I got my Peachie-Pie. I got her when Mr. M. passed. What will I do?"

"Go home, make a nice cup of tea, and watch one of your murder mysteries. I'll stay in the clinic tonight. I'll call you in the morning. Come let's put this little gal in a kennel."

Weeping, Mrs. Miggins followed him to the overnight room and let her kiss her baby goodbye before shutting the tired animal in a pen. "Are you sure Peaches will be okay?" She twisted her hands together.

"I hope so. I'll do an ultrasound to be sure there's nothing else obstructing her throat. I'll let you know if anything changes." The dog was fine. The drumstick bone was intact and had no sharp edges. He prayed Mrs. Miggins was scared enough to modify her behavior. He hated seeing her upset, but she needed to realize what she was doing was terrible for Peaches' health.

It was unfortunate that he was sending her home scared, but after three years of arguments, he was fed up. A serious jolt of fear might help her learn her lesson. Eventually, he calmed Mrs. Miggins enough to go home. He did a complete exam on Peaches and settled the tired pup back into the kennel. As he closed the door, he remembered his ringing phone.

He pulled it out and checked the screen. Tyson had called but hadn't left a message. That wasn't a good sign. A call that close to midnight meant something serious was up. He called his brother back.

"Hey, Ty, What's up? Sorry I didn't answer, I was with a patient." Tyson grumbled about nothing in particular for a few minutes. He had something on his mind and was having trouble getting to the point.

Tyson was great with sports, he dealt well with kids, parents, and teachers, but discussing anything emotional or close to his heart always tripped him up.

"I'm finished with my patient. Why don't you swing by for a brew?" He climbed the inside stairs between his clinic and the oversized apartment above it. The clinic had been custom built in the early 2000s and had a five-bedroom apartment over it. The designer, the previous vet, had three kids and wanted lots of space. Behind the clinic was a large yard, complete with garden, sandbox, and play structure.

The entire thing sat amidst twenty acres of trees, five miles from town.

Zander didn't need the enormous apartment. He barely used half the space and kept the doors closed to three empty bedrooms to keep the echoes down and save heating and cooling the entire space. Eventually, he hoped to raise a family here, but that was a good five years in the future. If he ever found time to date. Heather's smile popped into his head. Nope. Not dating his brother's employee. He wouldn't, even if he had the time. That was a bear trap waiting to snap on his hand.

Derrick had taken him aside after dinner and warned him off Heather. His brother made it clear; Heather was off limits. His stomach still ached from the vicious elbow she'd given him.

The stairwell from the clinic opened up into his main entry, where outside stairs came up the back of the building. He flipped open the deadbolt on the main door and shucked his boots. His clothing had a bit of dog hair on it, hazard of the job, so he flipped them into the laundry and changed before grabbing a couple beer and a bag of all-dressed chips. Tyson's jock days might be over, but he still worked out and was always hungry.

A vehicle pulled in and uneven footfalls climbed the stairs. Ty knocked twice and let himself in. The beauty and curse of family was that they came and went as they pleased. Especially Tyson with whom he was closest.

"In the living room," he called out rather than getting up.

Shoes thumped on the floor, and Ty padded over in his sock feet. "Bro."

"Bro."

Zander flipped up the footrest of his favorite recliner and leaned back. Ty would talk when he was ready. His brother flopped onto the matching leather couch and raised his own footrest. They drank in silence. Half a beer later, Zander said, "What's up?"

"Nothing." Tyson grabbed the chips and opened the bag. He offered it to Zander, who shook his head, then Ty started munching.

"Didn't you get enough dinner?" Obviously not, but it was a conversation opener.

"Nope. But it was good." He loudly chewed a few more chips. "Does it ever bug you?"

"Being invited over for a delicious dinner cooked by a pretty woman? Nope. I could do that all day."

"You should totally go for that. She's hot, but not my type."

"You have a type?" No way was he getting into a discussion about Heather. He shouldn't have mentioned her at all.

He waited for a response. Spending time with Ty was an acceptable substitute for his usual evening pastime of sitting on his balcony, studying the stars, and pondering his family's problems.

"Heather's too bubbly and outgoing. I need someone reserved and quiet. Someone who won't mess with my reputation as a high school principal."

"What's your point?"

"Doesn't it get to you? Watching Jacob and Lexi? All cute and cuddly and in love." He sneered the last word. "And Mom? Pushing women at us?"

"Bro. You got an issue with love? I'm thrilled that Jacob found someone. Lexi helps him relax. They're good together. I think everyone deserves love."

Ty snorted in derision. "But Mom? And the dates? No, thanks."

"I thought you wanted to date."

"There isn't a single woman in this town who I would trust my career with. It grates on my nerves that I can't find someone wholesome. Women throw themselves at me all the time. They think I'm rich from my years as a quarterback."

"You are."

"No, I'm comfortable. That money is my retirement fund. I work for my day-to-day expenses. I don't need a woman coming along and trying to spend all that. Or worse yet, trying to get me into her bed like I'm some kind of status symbol."

"Is that why you were so quiet at dinner? You're jealous of Jacob and Lexi's happiness? There's someone out there for you too."

"Not in this town. Why do you think I hit the city every few weeks? I'm not getting any younger. I go to see women I've met online. To see if anything clicks. So far none of them have knocked it out of the park for me." He sighed and chugged his beer. He hopped up and headed for the kitchen. "Want another?"

"Sure, why not." Zander drained his bottle and handed it over. "You dating these women or something more earthy?"

"Dating. Life's too short for screwing around." He returned with the beer and a roll of garlic sausage. He broke off a two-inch chunk and tossed it at Zander and then broke off another for himself.

Their mother would pitch a small fit at their caveman manners, but he knew enough to confine his rough behavior to men only events like this one. There was something freeing about being able to relax and be himself.

"Cool. Good luck with finding the right woman." He meant the words and hoped he didn't sound sarcastic.

"I'm thirty-two. It's time to get on with my life. My jock days are over. I want to find a good woman and start having a family before the goods dry up."

His utter sincerity shocked Zander. "Guess it's too late for me. I'm thirty-eight." He laughed, but his brother's words echoed in his head. Was it time to seriously think about his own future instead of fretting about his mother and siblings? He did want a family, eventually, because he certainly didn't want to end up alone like Mrs. Miggins with nothing but an overweight dog for company.

Again, his mind circled around to Heather and the impossibility of dating her. She's your brother's employee, he reminded himself. She had shadows in her eyes too, and he didn't need to be responsible for solving someone else's problems. Darn it, now he sounded selfish, even to himself.

Everyone had a history and often that meant wounds. His father's death had left scars. Watching his mother grieve had hardened his heart. He didn't want to live that. Ever. Being alive when such a big piece of your heart was gone. No, thank you. Even so, sometimes, late at night, he wished he had someone to draw into his arms when the darkness and solitude grew oppressive.

He shelved his confusing, circular thoughts, and tried to help Ty through his troubles. Unfortunately, hearing about his brother's longings had sparked something in himself that he didn't want to identify, or deal with.

Chapter 7

"Good morning," Zander greeted Lexi as he strolled into the inn.

"Zander, you're up and about early."

Her smile was warm and welcoming, unlike the water pouring down from the heavens. It had been raining for three days straight. He was more than sick of it and tired of sitting at home avoiding his thoughts.

"I thought I'd swing by and make sure my brother was still treating you right." He winked and she laughed.

"Liar. What really brings you here? I suppose you'll tell me that you're not here to see Heather. I saw you watching her at the opening and again at dinner the other night. She's very pretty."

He pretended to consider what she said. "She's okay." He'd take the teasing from Lexi. From the day she showed up as the inn's first, unexpected guest, they'd shared a casual friendship.

"Okay. You crack me up. She's stunning." She rolled her eyes. "And man, can she cook. I'm going to weigh a million pounds from all the treats."

"She can bake, that's for sure. Dinner the other night was pretty good too," he conceded. *Except that slapping bit, but he'd deserved it.*

"I'm so glad she'll be expanding our food service. It's going to be great for business." She gave him a sly look. "Want to grab coffee and a muffin with me? I was just going to take a break." She didn't wait for an answer, she just waved him toward the kitchen.

"That sounds great. I could use a coffee. It's cold and depressing out there." And seeing Heather's sweet smile was the perfect antidote to the weather.

"Morning, Heather," Lexi called out. "Is there coffee?"

Heather turned and smiled. "There's always coffee. No better way to start the day." She seemed to notice Zander. "Hi, Zander. How are you?" She whirled round and grabbed two mugs and set them by the coffee pot then turned her attention to whatever she was mixing.

"I'm good. How's your world?" The bright florescent lights shone on her blonde hair turning it to molten gold with streaks of liquid silver.

"Same old, same old. I cook, I do dishes, I go home and sleep." Her laugh brightened the room and tickled across the hairs on the back of his neck like a whisper soft touch, leaving longing in its wake. *Whoa!*

Heather worked quietly while he and Lexi drank their coffee. "Can you do me a favor?" Lexi asked. "I need some birthday supplies from the mall. Do you think you could run and get them for me? Jacob's gone to Seattle for the day, and Derrick is busy fixing a busted radiator. I'm swamped at the desk." She clasped her hands together in entreaty. "Please?"

"I guess." He wasn't much of a shopper. He was a get in, get out, kind of guy. "Do you have a list?" His clinic was closed today, except for emergencies. He had time to run an errand or two.

"Oh. I need muffin papers, parchment, and more measuring spoons. Could you grab those for me?" Heather asked eagerly.

"You should go with him," Lexi said with a smart-alecky grin. "Get my stuff, and your stuff, and look at ideas for decorating the inn for the July long weekend. I haven't gotten that far in planning a celebration yet. This would be a huge help for me."

"I have to cook," Heather said, denying the request without actually saying no.

"Oh, poo. Breakfast is over. There are enough treats to last until tomorrow. You can spare the time."

Heather winced.

"Consider it an order from your boss. I'll grab my list." She scooped up her muffin and coffee and quickly stepped out of the kitchen.

"I guess we're going shopping." Zander laughed.

"I guess."

"Wow. Bank that overwhelming enthusiasm," he teased. "Don't you like shopping?" It was probably more that after he stole that kiss, she wasn't his biggest fan. He wanted to regret kissing her, it was wrong. But somehow, he couldn't find the remorse he should feel.

"Something like that. Let me finish up here and we can go. The sooner we leave, the sooner it's over and done."

Lexi returned and handed Zander her list and the inn's credit card. "Use this to pay for my stuff, and whatever Heather needs for the kitchen. You kids have fun now." Laughing, she walked away. Why did people in love think everyone else wanted to be hooked up?

They drove to a mall in Richmond, and it was a zoo. Stores were packed and kids were running everywhere. "Remind me not to go shopping on the weekend," he groused five stores in.

"Me too." She scooted toward him to make room for a wide stroller to pass by. "This is nuts."

Zander laughed at the absolute frustration in her voice. "Was there anything else you wanted to do while we're here? I mean, since we're here anyway, we might as well get all our jobs done."

"I wouldn't mind hitting the bookstore. The one in town doesn't have what I'm looking for. But I've got all these bags so we should probably just go."

"I'll run the bags to the truck and meet you in the bookstore. I've got time and bookstores are the one store I don't detest."

"Are you sure?" Her uncertain look was adorable.

"One hundred percent. Give me those." He wrestled the bags from her hands. "Back in ten. Meet you there."

♥♥♥

He was gone before she could formulate a response. She strode past a few stores into the massive chain bookstore. Smaller bookstores especially used ones, were more her style, but she wanted to find Jeremy Osten's new cookbook. It was supposed to be a combination of recipes and a biography. Their local store had sold out the day it was released and didn't have more copies yet.

She strolled the aisles pausing to look at the trinkets and notebooks. She did love a pretty notebook. She picked up one with flowers and cookies on the cover. It would be perfect for her recipes. She found a sweet romance from her favorite author before she hit the section she was looking for. Bookstores were hard on her budget. She did some mental math to ensure the costs were within the amount she set for fun things.

She was paging through the book when she sensed someone looking at her. She cast a quick peek to her left. Zander stood at the end of the next aisle watching her.

"What are you doing? That's creepy," she chided. It wasn't. There was a light in his gaze that shifted something close to her heart.

"Sorry. I didn't want to interrupt you. You were enthralled." He grinned. "I've got what I needed. How about you?"

"Thanks for waiting. I think I'm good. Let's pay and get out of here." They had to ease between people to reach the register. She paid first and stood waiting for him. His stomach growled.

"What was that?" she teased.

"Wasn't me. Must have been you. I can tell you're starving. Maybe I should feed you."

"Oh," she raised her voice to make it a question. "I'm the hungry one? I see. Well then, you should probably feed me. I could use a snack before we head back."

"Restaurant or the food court?" he asked.

"Food court!"

"You're a chef and you want to eat at the food court?"

"Absolutely! I love a good greasy feast now and then. Don't you?" She nudged him with her elbow.

He slung his arm over her shoulder. His arm was the perfect height to go around her, and he smelled incredible. *She was in so much trouble*. She needed to keep her distance.

♥♥♥

"What do you feel like?" he asked when they reached the edge of the food court.

"Oh, fries from Fry Guys for sure. They make the best fries in the state. A burger and maybe a shake as well. How about you?"

"I can live with that. Shall we divide and conquer?"

"Absolutely. I'll get the burgers and shakes. You're on fry duty. I wanted the loaded fries with the works."

He gave her his order and they split up. Seven minutes later, they regrouped at a table for two. They ate in silence, enjoying every bite.

"Zander Bellamie, as I live and breathe," a voice carried across the food court. A rotund gray-haired woman hurried toward him.

"Brace yourself," he whispered. Louder he said, "Mrs. Jepson, so nice to see you."

Mrs. J dropped into a seat at the adjacent table. "How are you, son?"

"I'm great. Busy, but that's the status quo. How are you?"

She fluttered her hand. "Wonderful. My daughter is moving back to town. I can't wait to have you both over for dinner. You are still single?"

He choked on his drink. "Um. Yes. But I'm much too busy to date."

Mrs. J totally ignored Heather and patted his hand. "Well, since you're single, I look forward to seeing you at dinner. You'll adore my daughter. Tell your mother I said hello." She leaped up and power walked away.

"Wow." Heather laughed. "She's something."

"She's Mom's neighbor. I do not want to date her daughter, or anyone at this point. How do I get out of this?" He paused. His earlier idea returned full force. "I don't suppose you'd be willing to pretend we were dating. Would you?"

Her laughter shocked him. It rang out, ringing off the high ceiling and echoing around the large open space. People turned to stare, and smile.

"What's so funny? I'm serious." He'd thrown the idea out for consideration, but her amusement hurt. He massaged the ache in his forehead caused by her mirth.

"After you told your entire family about my fear of cats, you want to date?" She made air quotes around date and started laughing again. Finally, after an embarrassingly long time, she calmed. "You're hilarious, Zander. Danged funny."

"Are you saying no?" He tried not to frown.

"I'm saying I'll think about it. Although frankly, I don't see what's in it for me." She chuckled again. "Not that you aren't good company. But I recall something about your brother and castration."

"Well, it didn't hurt to ask." They'd talked a few times at the inn, and he enjoyed her company. They were more than acquaintances, but not quite friends. Why couldn't getting to know each other be part of dating? More importantly, why did it seem so imperative that she agree?

Chapter 8

Heather was up with the birds, despite it being her day off. Accustomed to being up early to start breakfast every morning, the habit was too ingrained to break. She didn't even need an alarm clock.

Last night she'd spent two hours listening to Quinn arguing with her boyfriend in the middle of the night. It didn't matter, her internal clock said it was time to get up. She slipped into some hot pink yoga pants and a T-shirt, grabbed her debit card, and snuck out the door. The morning was bright, but chilly.

The perfect day for a jog. She certainly wasn't a fitness freak. Her relationship with fitness was on-again, off-again. She worked out because she had to, not because she liked it. In the far distance, a lawn mower droned. Fluffy white clouds skittered across the sky on a wind that didn't reach the ground. It was a beautiful day. The clear sky promised heat and sunshine. A perfect day.

After stretching she ambled down the street and after a few blocks broke into a light jog. Nothing serious, just enough to get her heartrate up. She worked out twice a week on her days off. Always Mondays, and another day she scheduled at random, depending on who else was working in her kitchen. Okay, the inn's kitchen.

It wasn't the kitchen she'd envisioned owning when she dumped her money into her thieving ex's plan to open the next great thing in fusion cuisine, but it was well stocked and had top quality appliances. She controlled it, within set guidelines, so it felt like hers. It wasn't as good as owning her own place, but it was satisfying.

She smiled as she jogged along the beach. The salty tang of sea water hung in the air. It was such a change from city smog that she stopped to enjoy it and watch the waves roll in.

The phone in her pocket rang and she pulled it out. Marv! What could he want? She didn't care. Nothing he could say to her mattered. They were over. She hit decline and pocketed the phone. Her smile threatened to slip. She increased her pace and ran through the playpark. She wasn't going to let him ruin her day.

She had intended to take a short jog and head to the Tide's In Café for a latte but with her dark thoughts she reconsidered. She pushed on, leaving the beach. She jogged faster and faster until there was nothing left but the sound of her feet on the pavement and the thrumming of her blood in her ears. Her entire being was focused on putting one foot in front of the other. Running helped purge the demons chasing her.

She pushed harder. Faster. Longer strides. Marv's gloating face kept popping back into her mind. There was no escaping him. She gave one more push, giving her legs everything she had left.

Willing Marv's face to disappear but still running, she closed her eyes for a fraction of a second as she rounded the last corner onto Ocean Drive, the center of Half Moon Bay's retail sector and home to the café.

"Whoa!"

She heard the familiar voice and crashed into something solid. She teetered backward and rocked on her heels. Her eyes flew open as strong hands grabbed her arms and held her upright. She let out a yelp. She wasn't expecting anyone to be out this early.

"Zander!"

"Wow, you were really bookin' it. You nearly knocked me over."

His hands lingered on her arms, cool against the heat of her exertion. Strangely, they seemed to heat her up more than running had.

"Everything okay?" He looked behind her as if searching for someone chasing her.

"I'm good." She shifted back far enough that his arms dropped to his sides. She missed the contact instantly. "Just out for a run," she panted between words, trying to catch her breath.

"With your eyes closed?" he teased.

She rolled her eyes. "Just for a fraction of a second. Wasn't my brightest idea." Bending forward from the waist she rested her hands on her knees as she struggled to breathe. His giant dog sat on the sidewalk to his left. Not moving, just looking at her with his tongue hanging out.

"Is he going to eat me?" she asked, backing away a step.

Zander's laugh tickled her heart. "King? No. He won't hurt you. He's an old softie, and he's trained to sit when I stop walking. He won't go anywhere until I tell him to."

"Um. That's good."

"You look beat. Can I buy you a coffee?" His voice was welcoming and concerned. She was pleased that he didn't mention her obvious fear of animals.

"No need for you to buy, but if you're going toward the café, you can walk with me. I'm headed for coffee before cooling off on the walk home." She got the words out without too many gasps as her heart rate slowed.

He nodded. As he turned to walk beside her, she realized that he hadn't been headed for the coffee shop, he'd been going the opposite way. He snapped his fingers and King, fell in step on Zander's opposite side.

"What are you up to this early?" She glanced at him from the corner of her eye. Even from the side, his face was pinched and worried.

"Walking."

"Well, thank goodness. For a moment there, I thought you were levitating down Ocean Drive." She chuckled to let him know she was teasing in case he missed it in his preoccupation.

"Funny." He said dryly. They walked half a block before he spoke again. "Do you ever have those thoughts that just won't quit? The ones that wake you up and make you crazy?"

"Who doesn't? Why do you think I'm out here at the butt-crack of dawn?" She couldn't stop the slightly sarcastic response. His bark of laughter startled her and left her wanting to hear more. They walked another five hundred yards. At this rate, they'd be at the coffee shop before she knew why he was out here, if he spoke at all.

"So," she blurted, "about the thoughts you mentioned?" she paused, leaving him an opening to tell his tale. Another hundred yards and she couldn't stay quiet. "Today's a bad day for me. I wish I had work to distract me."

"You and me both. The clinic is closed Sunday, except for emergencies. What's bothering you?" The concern and interest in his eyes when he looked at her prompted her to speak.

"It's an anniversary of sorts."

"Not a good one, from the sound of your voice." They passed two shops. "I'm a good listener if you want to get something off your chest."

"Thanks." It was her turn to delay speaking. Finally, she managed, "My mom died when I was three. Dad died when I was in university. My sister Ava and I inherited everything. It wasn't millions, but it was a significant amount. Last year, I was in love. I believed that he loved me. Turns out he was only after the money." Her stomach cramped and her jaw clenched. Just thinking about screwing up and trusting Marv made her angry. Today is the one-year anniversary of finding out that he's a cad and a cheat.

"I think betrayal has to be the worst feeling."

She snorted. *Understatement of the year.* She was surprised to find herself offering details of her past. "Marv and I were opening a restaurant together. We found a location and I dumped every penny I had into it. We planned and organized for nearly a year. I paid for the renovations, the permits, and equipment. So much equipment." She sighed. "Anyway. We were basically engaged. At least I thought we were. Two weeks before the opening, this crazed, hugely pregnant woman shows up and starts screaming at me."

"You're kidding. I think I know where this is going," he sympathized.

"His wife. He was freaking married while we were dating." She kicked a small stone. It skittered half a block before coming to rest beside a lamp post. "I don't know if they planned it together, or if she was as surprised to find me there as I was when she showed up."

"Brutal. What did you do?"

"What else could I do? I kicked him in the nuts and left."

"Good for you! He deserved that and more. Did you get your money back?"

"Ha! I wish. I was stupid and in love. I didn't ask for a contract. Why would I need one? We were getting married. Or so I thought. I just spent my money on the things we needed. Or as it turned out, on the things *he* needed."

"No way. The man's a liar and thief, and an idiot if he didn't love you. There has to be a way to get it back."

"That would take a lawyer and the money is all gone. Hundreds of thousands of dollars. It took me nearly a year to find a decent job, so legal action is out of the question. I can't spend what I don't have, and no lawyer worth his salt would work without at least a retainer. I'm hooped. I just have to let it go and build a new nest egg. If only forgetting were as easy as it sounds." She kicked the stone again. It bounced off a trash can and hit her in the shin.

Stupid karma.

"How did you end up in Half Moon Bay?"

"Pure sweet luck. When I couldn't pay my rent and lost my apartment, I was rooming with a guy I went to school with. He was booked to cater for the inn's opening. He came down with a bug and asked me to fill in. He's one of the few chefs left that didn't fall for Marv's blackballing of me. Somehow, against the odds, I managed to impress your brothers and secure myself a job."

"A well-deserved job. I've been sneaking cookies and muffins from the kitchen almost every day since you started and the dinner you cooked for our family was incredible. I'm sorry you were used and hurt like that. Your ex is an idiot."

"Thanks." His simple words took some of the sting out of Marv's betrayal, but she knew it would be a long time before she fully trusted another man. She had a rock-solid contract with Derrick, one she'd asked for and that he'd happily provided. It protected them both. But on a personal level, there were no contracts or guarantees and she wasn't ready to risk her heart again.

Chapter 9

Zander was surprised by how angry he was at Heather's story. Her past explained the glimmers of sadness he saw in her eyes. Who did that to another person? He'd like to find this Marv guy and give him a beating. He wanted to pull Heather into his arms and make everything right for her. Not being able to do either was emasculating.

"I can't get your money back, but I can treat you to a coffee," he offered.

He took two fast steps and stepped into the café's alcove entry and pulled open the door, holding it for Heather to enter. "After you." He bowed and waved her forward. "King, stay." The dog moved to the left of the opening and lay down in the shade beside a small fountain with a sign declaring it a "Doggie Fountain."

"Thanks." Her smile was weak, like she couldn't shake off the past.

They paused a few steps inside the door to scan the sandwich board displaying the day's specials. The shop smelled like heaven. Coffee, bacon, melted cheese, and fresh baking lingered in the air, making him drool. "The bacon and egg wrap looks good," he said.

"It does. I think I'll have that and a French vanilla latte. Oh, and a glass of water." He didn't think she was asking him to order her meal or pay for it. She was much too independent for that, but he stepped forward and ordered for both of them before she could object.

He winked at her as he tapped his card. "This one's on me. The next one is on you."

She frowned. After a second, she nodded. "Fair enough. Next one is on me. But can we walk while we eat? If I don't cool down properly, I'll be too stiff to walk tomorrow."

"Sure, but you ordered a glass of water."

She raised a pink floral water bottle that matched her hot pink leggings and T-shirt. He'd been so wrapped up in Heather he hadn't noticed she carried anything. "I'll fill this up and I'll be good to go."

Five minutes later, food and drink in hand, they headed out, King walking along with them. Heather carried her sandwich in one hand, her coffee in the other and had her freshly filled water bottle tucked under her left arm.

"The clinic is outside of town. How did you end up here?" she asked and dove into her spicy egg wrap.

"Drove." He'd come to talk to Tyson about his growing feelings of needing to move on with his life but hadn't worked up the courage yet.

"You drove. Haha. Funny. I bared my soul to you. It's your turn."

He wasn't sure he wanted to open up to a woman he was just getting to know. "Family." A single word was all he managed.

"You've got a great family. Everyone is nice, though Derrick is a bit gruff. I like your mom. Her heart is enormous."

"Yeah, she's great. I worry about her since Dad passed. You know, does she take on too much when she should get one of us to do things for her? Is she lonely? Is she happy?"

109

"You could ask her," Heather suggested.

He took three swallows of his coffee. "She'd be evasive and try to distract me. She's not a liar, but I don't think she'd be completely honest. I'm sure she feels like she needs to protect us, but she's getting on in years and needs more help than she's willing to admit."

"And that worries you."

He appreciated her understanding. "And Derrick? He's bent on killing himself on that stupid bike. Tyson's got something going on he doesn't talk about, but he's afraid of getting old without having a family. I feel like I need to set him up with a nice woman, but he'd never go for that. Mom does more than enough date pushing. Jacob still works too hard, but at least I can relax a bit about him now that he's got Lexi. Poor Ella is hurting so badly about losing her mother, though she's happier now that Lexi's entered the picture." He felt silly for blurting out his family woes, but Heather was easy to confide in.

"It must be difficult to have so many people to worry about." She tossed her wrapper in a trash can stylized to resemble an octopus and placed her hand on his arm. She squeezed lightly, stealing his breath.

He cleared his throat. "Thanks."

"You're welcome."

He liked that she said the words rather than some quip like sure, or no worries. Those responses always struck him as insincere.

"And what about Zander? What does he need?" Like she had in the kitchen yesterday, she managed to turn his thoughts back on himself.

A simple question without a simple answer. He pondered it as they walked toward Johnson's Point, a cliff that overlooked the ocean. The high bluff was fenced in to keep people from tumbling off the one-hundred-foot drop. It was his favorite daytime thinking spot. He loved the extra tang of salt in the air and the pounding of waves against the rocks. On windy days, you'd get salt spray in your face. "I have no idea what I need," he lied.

He sat on a picnic table with his feet on the bench. Heather sat beside him. Not touching, but close enough he could feel her heat. He was tempted to lean closer, but after kissing her in the kitchen he wasn't going to press his luck so soon.

"It's beautiful here. You can see for miles."

Far out in the ocean, enormous container ships inched past. Some headed north, some south. At this distance they looked like toys. A ship's horn blared. "Look, there," he pointed. "That's a Brandt's cormorant. Watch it dive." As if on cue, the bird dove soundlessly into the water and flew up again seconds later with a fish in its mouth. He almost envied its simple life. No complex relationships. Well except the part where cormorants mated for life. He wasn't ready to go there. Yet.

"They're incredible. Look!" She gestured wildly as a second cormorant dove and came up with nothing in its beak. "Oh, he didn't get anything." They watched the birds in silence.

"If you could do anything you wanted, what would it be?" Her question startled him. His mind was on birds, not his personal life.

He swirled the dregs of his coffee and stared out at the ocean. "That's the thing. I'm not sure I know. I love being a veterinarian. I love my family."

"I hear a but." She nudged him with her elbow. Awareness of her proximity, and her attraction sparked up his arm. He peeked at her. She wasn't looking at him, she was peering out to sea, yet somehow, he knew he had her entire attention. Attention without pressure to answer.

"Honestly, I never thought about it. It's tough feeling like the family patriarch. I don't know how my dad did it. I don't know how Mom handles the stress of worrying about so many kids."

"Are you the oldest child?"

"No. Jacob is oldest, then Derrick, then me. Tyson is the baby by several years."

"Oh, you said you feel like the family patriarch. I thought maybe that meant you were the oldest. I can see the oldest child feeling responsible. How did you end up carrying that load?" She took a sip of her latte and set the cup on the table beside her.

"Dad died five years ago. Derrick was serving overseas, and Jacob was a business tycoon in the city. Tyson was in his prime as an athlete and had just left the CFL for the NFL. I was working at a clinic in Dallas. I hadn't bought into the business; I was saving to open my own practice. That meant I was free to come home and watch over mom. She didn't need to be alone at a time like that. Lucky for me, the clinic here was up for sale."

"Do you regret coming home?" She had a way of getting right to the heart of the matter and asking questions he hadn't considered, at least not consciously. "Living in Half Moon Bay wasn't my plan. I hadn't really decided where I wanted to live."

"But you came home anyway. Because your family needed you."

"Initially, I took a leave of absence and came for the funeral. I intended to stay a couple months. But Mom was a wreck. She'd been with Dad since she was a kid. They'd known each other since grade school. She was devastated. I worried she'd slip into depression.

Buying the clinic and moving home seemed the right thing to do."

"Caring for a parent is a big burden."

Again, with the accurate aim.

"I thought it would be, but it wasn't. Mom struggled for a while, which is understandable, but she moved on with her life. There are still glimmers of sadness in her eyes at times, but I think overall she's become accustomed to the loss. At least as much as one can adapt to the loss of their other half." At that moment he recognized that Heather's shadows matched his mother's. They were mourning something they'd never get back. Was there anything besides time that could erase those shadows? Maybe a new love?

He didn't want to think about his mother with anyone but his father, but maybe it was time for her, and Zander to move on. Maybe with the sweet woman sitting beside him, easily making him bare his soul.

"Your mom is a very upbeat person. Perhaps she'll find a new man."

He nodded. It was startling how Heather's thoughts mirrored his own. This conversation was taking him places he didn't want to go but there was something freeing in talking to Heather, in sharing his problems.

"You know your family are all adults, right? Capable of making their own decisions and floundering after their mistakes? Why do you feel responsible? That's a big burden."

"It isn't a burden," he snapped. "They're my family. I love them." She didn't respond beyond a simple nod. There was no judgment or accusation in the silence. It was comfortable, almost as if she understood what he meant, but it grated on him anyway. "It's sometimes difficult to remember that they're responsible for themselves. I worry."

"That's what good brothers do. They worry, but they also let their siblings make mistakes and suffer the consequences of those mistakes." She patted his shoulder, her hand lingering for a few seconds.

"That sounds like the voice of experience. Do you have siblings?"

"I have a sister. She's a doctor in Nova Scotia. Ava is two years younger than me, and my only family."

"That sounds lonely."

Heather thought about it.

Was she lonely? Maybe a little. His companionship shone a spotlight on how few people she had in her life. Yet she didn't feel lonely while she was with Zander.

She wasn't lonely.

Was she?

Okay, maybe a little. Late at night when she woke alone with no one to turn to. Or when she had something to celebrate, like landing the job at the inn, or when she was worried about life's problems. Quinn was a great confidant, but it wasn't the same as being in a relationship with a man she cared about.

Dang it, she was lonely.

"I miss my parents. I don't miss my ex, but I miss being in a relationship. I have several good friends in Canada and a couple here. I'm alone, but not lonely. If that makes any sense." Heather picked up her coffee and swallowed the last few sips as her own words echoed in her mind. She wished she could believe them.

"I can see that," Zander said. "I work long hours. I've got the clinic and my rescue animals. My family gets together for dinner a couple times a week. That's good because it means I don't have to chase them down. I'm busy, and alone, but I don't often feel lonely."

A small frown formed between his eyes, and she wondered if he was telling the truth.

"Cool." *Stupid response, Heather.* "Ever wish you had someone to hang with, you know to go to the movies or out to dinner with? No pressure? Just a pal?" She found herself wishing he'd say yes. It was silly. This was his hometown. He probably had dozens of friends. He wasn't floundering around looking for his place like a fish out of water the way she was.

She could easily visualize herself spending time with Zander. He was a nice guy. He was kind, well-built, handsome. He had a lot going for him, not the least of which was how much he cared for his family. It struck her that he was ideal husband material. If she were looking, which she wasn't.

"Are you asking me out?" he teased.

She laughed. "No!" She elbow bumped him again, just because she liked feeling the heat of his arm against hers. It had a way of warming her right to her heart.

She watched him watching the birds instead of responding immediately to her question. She wondered if the idea made him uncomfortable. She hopped off the table and dusted off her backside. "Well, I should get home. Lots to do today." Nothing really, but he didn't need to know that. She picked up her empty cup and water bottle.

He glanced at his watch. "Me too. Yardwork. For me, and for Mom."

They walked briskly down Ocean Drive. Just before they got back into town, he said, "I was thinking about the idea of fake dating again. We could kill two birds with one stone. We could be friends and let everyone think we were dating. It would get Mom and her friends off my back and you and I could hang without pressure."

Her heart skittered. She had been thinking about fake dating Zander, entirely too much. The idea of hanging with him was more exciting than it should be. She shifted through the pros and cons of the idea. After Marv, she sure didn't want to date but it would be nice to have someone to do things with. Quinn was always busy with her boyfriend and didn't have much free time. The biggest risk was her job. There was a lot of uncertainty on how Derrick would react.

They walked along discussing the pros and cons of faking a relationship. Finally, she agreed to his crazy proposal of fake dating, with a few stipulations. There would be no kissing. The only public displays of affection would be limited to handholding and maybe an occasional hug. The hardest thing to reach an agreement on was keeping it from his brothers. She refused to risk her job for him.

Part of her wondered why she agreed. Maybe to combat her growing loneliness without risking her heart. They wouldn't be spending much time together.

Their acquaintanceship just became friendship with a fancy new label. At least that's what she was telling herself.

"I hope this works for you and doesn't blow up in our faces," she said.

"It'll work. If Mom thinks I'm dating, she'll stop shoving women at me. Trust me."

That was the thing, she did trust him. She tried not to worry. Maybe it would be okay. "Let me know when you want to hang out, boyfriend."

"Should I call you at the inn?" he asked.

"Oh gosh no." You heard Derrick the other night, he'd would go ballistic. "Let's trade numbers. Can I have your phone?"

He handed her the phone and she shot herself a text after adding herself to his contact list. "There. Now I have your number too." Not that she'd message him first. This whole fake dating idea was his, so if he wanted it to work, he'd figure it out and call her.

Still, as they walked back down Ocean Drive, something built in her chest that felt suspiciously like anticipation. Even so, a skitter of nervousness crept through her. Hopefully this wasn't one huge mistake.

Chapter 10

Heather bustled around her apartment getting ready to go out. "Have you seen my pink sneakers?" she asked Quinn who sat at the kitchen table painting her nails with clear, sparkle polish. The acrid smell burned Heather's nose. She'd always hated that odor.

"Aren't they in the back of the hall closet? What's up with you? You're all atwitter." She laughed. "Look at Heather. She's all twitterpated."

"Ha. Ha. I'm going to the antique market with Zander." She dropped to her knees and burrowed into the pile of shoes in the closet. "Got one!" She pitched one runner behind her and kept digging.

"Are you going on a date, or what? I thought you said you weren't going to date anyone for a while."

"I'm not. We're pretending to date. Look, I'm just trying to get used to trusting men again. It's a friendly thing. He's trying to keep his mother off his back." Her words made something shrivel in her heart. "I guess he's looking for a bedframe or something for his place.

He asked me to keep him company but warned me there might be a lot of walking. I need good shoes."

"What's wrong with your work shoes?" Quinn chuckled.

"I can't wear them with capris. They're black. My pants are fuchsia. I would look ridiculous. And what's with the laugh?" She leaned back to glare at her roommate.

"You crack me up. Since you moved in you've been telling me you aren't dating anyone until you get your life back on track. This is the third time you've gone out with Zander in the last week. That looks suspiciously like actual dating."

"We're *fake* dating. Neither of us has time for the real thing."

"And yet, you're going out," she paused dramatically, "again. I swear you spend more time with Zander than you would if you were actually dating the man."

Heather closed her eyes and took a deep breath. No sense snapping at Quinn. Especially since she was right.

"I'm telling you; it isn't real. If it were, he'd stop answering his phone when we were together. I swear that thing is superglued to his hand." She dug deeper in the closet, tossing things to the side as she tried to unearth her left shoe. "That phone goes off every five minutes. He left the movie three times on Friday. He kept rushing out to the lobby to take calls. Who gets that many calls?"

"Zander's a busy man. I'm sure some of it was veterinary emergencies. I know he dotes on his mother too."

"And his niece. Oh, got it!" She backed out of the closet and held her shoe up like a trophy. She pushed everything back into the closet and grabbed both sneakers and went to the table. She pulled on a socklet and her right shoe. "Can you believe we actually skipped dessert the other night because his niece called and needed a ride home from a friend's house."

She sighed. "The kid said, "I can't call Dad, I'm mad at him." Instead, she calls Zander, and he rushes to her aid. I could never date a guy like that. I'm not

125

dating. I'm hanging with a friend. Dates are out until I get my life reorganized."

"You've got a decent job now. That's a big step."

"Yes, I have a job. But I still need to rebuild my reputation, save a boat ton of money, and open my own shop. Being independent and running my own kitchen has been my dream since culinary school. Nothing, and no one is going to stop me from reaching that dream. Dating would interfere with those plans."

"Okay, so you aren't dating." Quinn screwed the cap back on the polish. "Explain to me why you've curled your hair, you're wearing mascara and lip gloss for a pretend date. You're wearing a new outfit and you're freaking out over shoes. You're dressing to impress, girl."

She dropped her shoe. "Holy crap. I am." Her mind flitted between panic and excitement. "Maybe I should cancel."

"Why?"

"Because I can't get serious about a man. That's not my plan. And you're right, I am trying to impress

Zander. He's a great guy. Kind, considerate. He opens doors for me. He's so ... chivalrous. I like him."

"So, spend time with him and see where it goes. Maybe it'll turn real." She laughed. "Or more real than it seems now, but it seems pretty real from this side of the table."

"I can't. I've got life plans. He's my boss's brother." Ten other reasons raced through her mind. "He isn't interested in real dating. He's too busy."

"You do know that life is what happens while you're making plans, right?" She reached out and patted Heather's hand. "Don't overthink it. You like him, he seems to like you. Why don't you run with it? See what happens."

"And when it goes south, and we break up? Then what? You know how the Bellamies are? They stick together. Jacob will fire me."

"Why? If your imaginary breakup doesn't impact your work, why would he fire you? You're grasping at straws, trying to find reasons why it won't work. What are you actually afraid of? Not all men are Marvin the Manipulator. Zander's a good guy. I've known him for years. Take a chance and if it goes to crap, deal with it."

"It's not that easy." Heather banked a sigh. Quinn was wrong. She didn't dare risk dating Zander. There was too much at stake.

"Love is never easy. Look at me." She waved at herself. "I've dated ten guys in the four years I've been in town. All of them bombed out, but I keep trying. Duke's not perfect, but I'm trying to make it work."

"I don't see why. You deserve better. You should dump him and find someone new." The door buzzer chimed.

"Saved by the bell," Quinn quipped. "Get going. Don't shut yourself off from the possibility of building something real with Zander. The heart wants what the heart wants."

"Fine." She tied her second shoe, grabbed her small backpack style purse and after hitting the speaker to let Zander know she was on her way, she raced downstairs. He stood beside the truck looking handsome and happy in his black jeans and pale green button-down shirt.

"Where are we headed?" she asked as she climbed into the truck through the door he had opened for her.

He closed the door and got in on his side before answering. "Well, I've already checked out Buried Treasures, they're a great antique shop, but they didn't have what I wanted. I thought we'd head to The Rusty Anchor. It's an antique market housed in an old canning factory just up the highway. A couple dozen vendors have stalls. It's like a cooperative. I'm hoping my friend will have what I need. It's only a twenty-minute drive right along the coast. Does that work for you?"

"Sure. I haven't explored much since I arrived. Work keeps me busy." Work, and the fact that she avoided driving whenever she could to save gas, kept her close to home.

"Excellent. I grabbed you a coffee and a croissant." He waved to the cupholder. A small bakery bag sat atop two coffee cups. "French vanilla latte, right?"

"Perfect. Thank you." He knew her coffee order. He must have taken note when they got coffee after her run. How sweet that he remembered.

He put the truck in gear and pulled away from the curb.

The morning sun warmed her through her window as they headed north. "It's a glorious day." She flipped open her coffee and inhaled the scent. "Why does coffee smell so delicious? Especially before the first cup."

"One of life's mysteries, I guess. I'm on my third coffee. I've been up since four. I had an emergency. A dog was hit by a semi. Luckily, he's going to be okay, it just nicked him."

"Speaking of dogs, where is yours?"

"I left King at the inn. Derrick's going to watch him."

"Cool." *Thank heaven.* The dog seemed nice, but he made her nervous. He was too big and too enthusiastic. "Are you sure you want to do this today? You aren't too tired? Maybe it would be better to wait until you're more rested."

"I'm about as rested as I get. I don't need much sleep." He flashed her a grin. "We're both off today and my friend Eric called to tell me he just got in a shipment of bed frames. I don't want to miss my chance to snag the right one. Besides, I don't want to cancel our date on short notice."

Date? He thought this was an actual date. What happened to friends who were faking it?

Quinn's voice popped up in her head whispering, "Take a chance. The heart wants what the heart wants."

There were five million things that could go wrong if she were dating Zander. Her mind skipped like a scratched record listing reasons not to date him. She could get her heart broken. They could have a huge fight. They might not be compatible. She could lose her job.

Her optimist side chimed in. She could fall in love. They could be happy together. He wasn't a lying cheat like Marv. It might be her chance to find true love.

Stop overthinking, Heather. Let it go for today and enjoy yourself.

"I'm happy we're still going, as long as you're not too tired to drive. If you are, I'm also good with rescheduling." She studied him while pretending to watch the scenery go past. He didn't look too tired. He seemed awake and alert.

"I promise, if I get tired, I'll ask you to drive."

"What? You'd let a woman drive your precious truck?" She clutched her chest in mock surprise. "Say it ain't so."

"Funny. Very funny." He chuckled. "Don't tell my brother, but I let Ella drive my truck on the back roads. She's pretty good. Of course, this truck's an automatic. She might have more trouble with a standard. She's not very tall."

"Jacob would have a fit if he knew."

"Probably. He tends to be overprotective of Ella. I'm helping her grow and learn new things." He sounded proud of himself, and of his niece.

Funny that he was going against his brother's wishes. From what she'd seen, Zander wasn't a rule breaker and overprotective of his family. She decided not to worry about it. It wasn't any of her business and Jacob would find out eventually.

She looked past him. A rock-strewn beach raced past the window. Sun glinted off tiny ocean waves making it shimmer as if diamonds floated on the surface. She slid her partially empty cup back into the holder and opened her window a few inches. She inhaled deeply.

"I don't think I'll ever get tired of fresh ocean air. It's not just the salt, it's the seaweed, the fish. I swear I can smell the damp sand." She sighed happily. "It's so different from the city. While I lived in Toronto, I never realized how much the air stunk. I'd go for walks and runs thinking I was getting fresh air."

"Are you liking Half Moon Bay?" he asked, slowing behind a semi, waiting for an opportunity to pass safely.

"I think so. I can't get used to people I don't know calling me by name. I was in The Whale and Oyster a couple days ago. Quinn and I went for dinner because she had a gift certificate to use up. The waitress knew who I was. I was stunned."

"Small towns are like that. It can feel like you're living under a microscope. You'll get used to it. When I was a kid, I hated it. Everyone was watching. I'd do something I shouldn't, and my parents would know before I got home."

"I'll bet that forced you to follow the rules."

He laughed and she turned away from the farms outside her window to look at him. He had the best smile. Soft, sexy, enticing.

"You'd think so," he said. "What it taught me was to be sneaky. If we were careful enough, we could hide just about anything. Once my friends and I mastered secrecy, we kept our youthful stupidity hidden. Until the time we accidentally set fire to an abandoned barn on the Wilkerson's land." He winced. "That one got me grounded for three months."

"Oh no! What happened?"

"We had to be about eleven. Maybe twelve. My friend Elton, he's a police officer now, found a magnifying glass. We were trying to light things on fire."

Heather laughed. "More than trying apparently."

Zander winced. "We lit a few leaves on fire. We played for hours. Lighting fires and putting them out. We extinguished the last fire and went home. We were young and stupid. We didn't put it out properly. The wind came up during the night. Luckily a passing motorist called the fire in before it got out of control."

"How did you get caught?"

"Guilt. I felt terrible for days. Eventually, I confessed. My friends were mad. Luckily, by the end of my grounding, they were over it. We're still friends. What about you? Did you ever get caught doing something you shouldn't?"

"Actually, no. Dad was an investment banker. We lived five miles from town and had a chauffeur pick us up and bring us home to our nanny. I led a very sheltered, boring life. Ava and I just hung out at home."

"Sounds lonely."

"You'd think so, but it was all we knew. I didn't mind much. I was quite a bookish kid. We did have 'playdates' now and then and the occasional sleepover with friends. It was a good life. We never wanted for anything." She struggled to explain how it felt. "Anyway, I was twenty-four when Dad died. I was whiling away time at university, taking classes, not even working toward a degree. I'd been going since I turned eighteen. I had at least thirty-one and two hundred level courses under my belt. All from a dozen different fields. Dad was starting to pester me about choosing a major, but nothing really interested me beyond learning. When he died, I was lost for a couple years. Mom died when Ava was a baby, and I was only three. Eventually, I went to culinary school and here I am."

"I suspect there's a lot more to it than that. I can see why you'd feel overwatched in Half Moon Bay."

"Ya, after Dad passed, I kind of went nuts. Doing nothing and everything. Running amok. Spending money like crazy. Not having someone watching my every move was liberating. Fortunately, I never really had a taste for alcohol or the desire to do drugs. I could have ended up in trouble. But I traveled a lot and wasted money on stupid stuff."

She smiled. "Once I decided to learn to cook, culinary school was incredible. It straightened me out. But I sure learned to like being my own person without the world watching me." She chuckled. "I loved the city and the freedom. Your little town is so vigilant, it scrapes on my nerves now and then."

"You get used to it. When I first came back, I felt like a teen again. After I proved myself responsible, people lost interest. I expect once you've been around for a while, they'll find someone new to watch. Fortunately, gossips have short attention spans."

"I certainly hope so!" She was tired of feeling like a fish out of water. Everyone noticed her and now that she was 'dating' Zander, they'd notice even more.

This was such a bad idea. So why did it feel so perfect?

Chapter 11

Zander didn't laugh at Heather's strong hope that the eyes of Half Moon Bay's gossips would move on. It was funny to him, but probably not to her. He understood exactly how she felt. He'd shuddered under those judgmental eyes when he returned home. Now, he barely noticed the gossips, except when they were trying to find him a date. Last week alone, three of his patients tried to hook him up with someone they knew. Two daughters, and one granddaughter. Nobody understood that he was content with his life as a bachelor caring for his family.

"How much further?" Heather asked.

"About five minutes. Why?"

"Curious. I'm excited to look at some old stuff." She paused. "I have a few of Dad's antiques in storage. I couldn't bear to part with them when I sold everything else. Ava and I decided to sell the house. Neither of us wanted it. It wasn't that big, but it was cold and lifeless. It always reminded me of a museum or mausoleum." She shuddered. "No, thank you."

"It's a shame you lost all that money."

"It infuriates me when I think of it. But the worst part was the betrayal. He broke my trust. We had a verbal deal, and he broke it. You said it the other day, betrayal has to be the hardest thing to get past. It makes trusting again difficult." She inhaled a calming breath and tried to push away her disillusionment. "The past is dead and gone and I'm making my way ahead. The fact that Marv blackballed me won't mean anything once I open my own place." She clamped a hand over her mouth. "You didn't hear that. Please, don't tell your brother I plan to leave."

"How soon?" He seemed curious, not judgmental of her plans.

"Likely years. I need to save enough money to open my own place. The inn pays well, but not as well as a trust fund."

"Years? Wow. In that case, it doesn't matter, does it. A lot can change in that length of time. Who knows where any of us will be in five years, or ten. Your secret is safe with me."

He slowed and turned on his signal light. "Two minutes now." He drove down a quaint street of brightly colored businesses and pulled into an enormous parking lot in front of a cinder-block building. The building had been painted a calming blue with rust trim. A six-foot-high sign proclaimed it Rusty Anchor Antiques. "And here we are."

Heather glanced around the parking lot. "Oh, look at that!" On the northern end of the lot, a huge tent covered an array of antique cars and trucks. "Those look amazing." She jumped out of the truck and looked at him. "Come on, time's a-wasting. Maybe we can look at cars later if we finish inside fast enough." She grinned, shut the door, and sprinted toward the building.

Zander jogged to catch up. She would have beat him inside except she paused to hold the door open for a mother with a baby in a stroller and two other kids in tow.

"You're fast," he said once they were inside. He blinked to help his eyes adjust to the interior lighting. It was like a tomb after the morning's bright sunshine.

"Maybe you're just slow." She nudged him with her elbow.

She'd done that a few times the day they shared coffee on the overlook. It left him feeling like a co-conspirator. Warmth surged through him. He slung his arm over her shoulder.

"Well, friend, where shall we start?" He pointed left. "Vendors with smaller items, China, jewelry, and such, are over there. Furniture is that way." He pointed right. "Everything else is in between"

"Why don't we look at what we're here for and get that out of the way first? Then we can snoop to our heart's content."

"Good plan." He urged her forward without removing his arm from around her. She was tall but short enough next to him that she fit well against his side and her sweet cookie scent was soothing. Yesterday, when he walked past the bakery, on the way to the post office, the scent of lemon and sugar brought her instantly to his mind.

"Eric's place is at the very back. He specializes in furniture." Several times on the way to Eric's Heather paused to admire something. Once it was a plush chaise lounge, the next it was a smoking table. A solicitor's bookcase and a Formica table with matching chrome chairs also caught her eyes. She had a wide eclectic taste. After every stop, he managed to find a way to get his arm around her again. Surprisingly, she allowed it.

"Eric, this is my friend, Heather. Heather, Eric." He made the introductions, and they shared some small talk for a moment. "Okay, show me this bed."

The bed had a tall curving frame with wrought iron spindles. It was in pristine condition. It looked almost new, but not reconditioned. It was mint and it was exactly what he envisioned for his master bedroom. His current bed was a double box spring and mattress. He wanted something larger and nicer. Something that felt more adult, instead of college student moving into his first place.

143

"It's lovely." Heather stroked the curved wooden headboard. Her approval was enough to convince him that he wanted it at any price. He almost recoiled from the thought. Why was her opinion of the bed enough to sway him into purchasing it?

"What are you asking for it?" Zander asked. They dickered for a few minutes and finally struck a mutually agreeable deal that included a complete bedroom suite.

"I'm just going to look at that shop," Heather said. "You guys go ahead and catch up." She wandered away before he could answer.

When she was out of earshot Eric said, "She's cute. Is she your girlfriend?"

"We're just friends. She works for Derrick."

"You had your arm around her when you walked up. That doesn't spell friend to me." Eric gave him a penetrating look that demanded answers.

"Seriously," Zander said. "We're just friends."

"But you'd like to be more. Dude, I've known you for decades. Maybe you can lie to yourself, but you can't lie to me."

144

"I don't know what I want. She's great company but I have responsibilities. My business, my family, my rescue animals. If we dated and things went bad, it might cause issues between her and Derrick. I don't want to be responsible for that. He's already threatened to castrate me." He paused. "Truthfully, we're fake dating, just to keep all the matchmakers off my back." He twitched at the thought of more blind dates.

"Dude, you are so done for."

"What's that supposed to mean?" Zander demanded.

"You like her. You want her, and you have no idea how to fit her into your life. Something's going to have to change. Mark my words."

"I told you, we're fake dating. She's nice, but I don't have time for a real relationship. She's getting over a tough breakup. It's convenient for both of us."

"Is it?" Eric raised one eyebrow.

Zander ignored the implied question and the smirk that followed it. He was not falling for Heather. Was he?

Chapter 12

Zander flexed his fingers. They were always stiff after a difficult surgery and today's was anything but normal. The last few days had been crazy. Cats with kidney disease, a horse with a broken leg, way too many animals hit by cars, all on top of a full regular workload. He was exhausted.

He sat at his desk filling out post-surgical paperwork on the neutering of a golden retriever which had nearly died twice during the procedure due to unexpected complications. He stretched and wiggled his aching feet. They brushed against King who was curled up under his desk snoring. The crazy mutt had a way of knowing when Zander needed comforting.

Now that his patient was safely in recovery, under his new assistant's careful watch, his mind was jumping from topic to topic. It kept flipping to the fact that three days had gone by without texting Heather. Keeping his distance was surprisingly difficult.

Their fake dating had gone so well he was hooked on her. He wanted to be with her twenty-four seven. It wasn't what he had planned. She was taking up too much of his time. He'd even skipped a family dinner to be with her. He knew that if he called, they'd go out, and he was barely able to resist. Twice, he found himself in his truck on the way to the inn, to visit her. Both times, he'd gotten out and stayed home.

Somehow, along the way, he'd forgotten she was Derrick's employee and that what they shared wasn't real. Fake dating, not actual dating, he reminded himself. They were just friends. She was long-term material, not the stuff of flings which meant, no matter which way he sliced it, she was not for him.

His heart shriveled a little.

He worked with his office door almost closed to reduce the noise drifting in from the front desk. Jenny loved to sing along with the radio, though her voice wouldn't win any awards. She wasn't terrible, but she never hit the high notes, despite trying way too hard and way too loudly. Today was twice as bad because his assistant joined in the off-key rendition of Corb Lund's *Truck Got Stuck*.

The music shut off abruptly. In an unnaturally loud voice Jenny called, "Mrs. Bellamie. So good to see you." The raised voice was her way of announcing unexpected or potentially unwanted visitors.

Zander typed the last few words in his report and hit save just as his mother strolled into his office without knocking. Her gray hair was mussed, but she was glowing.

"Oh, so you aren't dead," she greeted him and smiled. She rounded his desk and hugged him before taking the seat across from him. She leaned back and crossed her arms over her chest. "I called you three days ago, you never answered."

"Mom. Hi. I've been busy. How are you doing? You look great." She was fast losing her winter pallor. She'd traded her jeans for walking shorts and a sleeveless blouse. She'd started walking after his father died. It was her way of coping with the loss. Now, she walked every day without fail. He wished he had her dedication. "Did you walk out here?"

"No. Don't be silly. It's miles. I rode my bicycle."

"You have a bike? When did you get that?" Wearing a helmet would explain her mussed up hair.

"On the weekend. You'd know that if you called."

Direct hit to his guilt gene.

"Why haven't you called?"

He suddenly felt like he was in a battle, and she'd just fired a warning shot across his bow. He quirked one eyebrow. "Busy? Besides, you don't need me pestering you every day. Do you?" Jenny came in carrying two mugs of coffee. "Thanks, Jenny." She nodded and left, pulling the door closed behind.

"Alexander Gage Bellamie, I do not *need* you to check in on me, but I *want* you to. It's reassuring to know my children are well. You are well, aren't you? None of your brothers have heard from you either. Only Ella has."

"You're checking up on me?" This was a twist.

"Tyson called. He's concerned."

Zander resisted the urge to roll his eyes. In a matter of days, he'd gone from being barked at for keeping tabs on everyone to being chided for not checking on them. His family was nuts. "Mom. I'm fine. I'm busy. I do have a job."

"That's never stopped you before. What changed?" She gave him a look that said she knew he was keeping secrets.

"Absolutely nothing. Mom, I'm busy. I need to hire another vet, and probably another tech and more front staff. Half Moon Bay is growing, and tourist season has started. There's too much work for one man to handle."

"Indeed. And yet, I've heard, more than once, that you've been seen around town with a woman. How does that fit into your busy schedule? Or is that why you're busy?" She leaned forward in interest. "Tell me about her. Are you dating? Is it serious? Do I know her, or is she a tourist?" She threw the questions out like a boxer throwing punches.

It was barely tourist season, though they'd be flocking to town in droves by July long weekend. "Mom!" His voice rose in exasperation, and he had to take a breath to relax. "I bumped into a woman I know when I was out for a walk. We walked together and talked."

"Oh, Heather. I heard you'd been in the café together and then were seen walking on the bluffs." She pinned him with her best 'fess up stare. "I heard you told Alma Stagling that you were dating. Of course, you never mentioned it to any of your family."

"Okay, Heather and I are dating." He fumbled for a way to make it sound legit. "I didn't tell you because it's new. We aren't serious. Yet. I didn't want to get your hopes up." *Or his.*

"Wonderful! Heather is a lovely girl. She'd make a nice wife for you."

"Heather would make a nice wife for anyone, but I am definitely not looking for a wife. Tyson needs a wife, why don't you find him a date?"

A picture of Tyson and Heather locked in an embrace flashed into his mind. It hit like a foot to the nuts. The idea of Heather with anyone but him made his hackles rise and his stomach clench. Tyson was not the right man for Heather.

"I have been trying to set him up, believe me." She gave him a sly smile. "You and Heather make a great couple and your babies will be adorable." She sipped her coffee with an air of satisfaction like she'd just arranged world peace. She made no bones about wanting more grandchildren, but this was ridiculous.

"Mom. Don't even start. We're barely dating. Hardly more than friends. We don't know where it's going. So, we're keeping it quiet. I'm pretty sure Derrick doesn't want me near her. Can we just keep this between us for now?"

"Fine." A mother's *fine* was worse than a girlfriend's *fine*. Her acquiescence wouldn't last long. Her frown was both admonishing and understanding.

Time to divert her from the topic. "When did you get a bike?" he asked.

She squinted at him. How was it that mothers could express so much with just a twist of their lips and pinch of their brows? "Last weekend. Ella and I went to Seattle. Didn't she mention it to you? We both got bikes. I thought it would give her a degree of independence if she didn't have to beg for a ride all the time. While we were there, I decided I wanted one too. You never forget how to ride. I only fell off once."

"You fell off your bike." He leaped up, spilling his coffee down his shirt. He slammed the mug on the desk and hurried to her side. "Are you okay? Did you break anything?" He reached out to examine her, but she slapped his hand away.

"I'm fine. Just a bit of chipped paint and a scraped elbow." She twisted in her chair and flashed him her left arm. It was scraped from the top of her elbow almost to her wrist.

"Ouch. That must have hurt." He winced. It was cleanly scabbed over, so he didn't annoy her by trying to examine it any closer.

"Road rash hurts much worse than I remembered. But I've got my balance again and it's amazing to ride around. I get to places much faster now. I've even got a basket and those little saddlebag things for carrying groceries."

"Panniers? This I have to see."

She followed him outside. It made him a bit crazy to think about his mother riding around town and down the quiet highway on a bicycle. She could fall off at any second and be seriously injured.

Outside, parked to the left of the clinic door was a shiny silver and red bike. It had a red wire basket, and red leather panniers. He recognized the brands. She hadn't gone cheap. Good for her. She deserved nice things.

"Nice bike. I do worry about you riding," he confessed.

"Don't fret. I'm pretty good. Let me show you how well I ride." She donned her helmet and hopped onto the bike with the energy of a twenty-year-old. She circled the nearly empty parking lot, laughing gleefully as she swerved here and there.

"Look, Zander, no hands!" She clapped as she rode. It took ten years off his life when she let go. She was even able to steer slightly without touching the handlebars. She screeched to a stop beside him and hopped off. It took a full minute to get his heart rate back to normal.

"I have to admit, you're pretty good."

"Did I ever tell you that I was in a bicycle trick riders club when I was young? Not quite today's bike parks with all the jumps and switchbacks, but I was pretty good. We called ourselves the Half Moon Riders. We rode in every parade. I could go half a block with my front wheel off the ground. I missed this." Her face glowed with excitement.

"That's amazing. I had no idea." Her happiness lifted some of his worry. She looked ten years younger. He wouldn't stop fretting about her riding around, but she certainly knew what she was doing.

"I'll show you pictures from back then, tonight after dinner. The entire family is coming. Do I need to invite Heather, or will you?"

"We're trying to keep this quiet, Mom."

She made a dismissive sound. "Bring her as a family friend. I'm off to the inn now. Give Heather a call and invite her. I'll follow up when I see her." She checked the buckle on her helmet and rode away with a fluttery wave of her fingers.

"Watch for cars!" he hollered at her retreating back. "Holy crap. My mother on a bike."

156

"No kidding. She's a dynamo," Jenny said from behind him. "I can't believe it."

"Me either. I better get a bell, and a headlight, and taillight for that thing. She walks at night. She'll probably ride at night too. Maybe a reflective vest."

Jenny laughed. "You do that." She smirked. "And don't forget to ask your *girlfriend* to dinner."

"Don't even start. Heather and I are fake dating to keep the old biddies off my back. I don't have time for a real relationship." He didn't hesitate to tell her the truth, and he'd long ago stopped chiding Jenny for eavesdropping. She never repeated what she heard. For his receptionist, knowing was more important than sharing. "There's nothing serious between us."

"Keep telling yourself that boss. Keep telling yourself that." Chuckling, she went back inside, leaving him staring after her. Jenny saw way more than she should.

He called after her. "Forget it, Jenny. All that courting and wooing? No, thank you." He said the words, even though they felt like a lie. He should probably be worried that being with Heather was nothing but a pleasure.

Chapter 13

After days of not hearing from Zander, Heather had concluded that he'd decided to end their fake relationship. It should have been a good thing. She didn't want any kind of relationship with a man, but she'd agreed to his crazy plan anyway. Something about Zander Bellamie was compelling and comfortable. She felt like they'd really connected over their "dates" and when they'd both shared deeper thoughts on the overlook. For a short while they'd been more than friends. They'd shared an emotional intimacy that touched her heart. Apparently, that feeling was one-sided since he seemed to be standing her up.

She banked a disappointed sigh. Their dating wasn't real. There was no reason to expect him to treat her like his girlfriend. She closed her eyes and breathed deeply to ease the tension in her chest.

Four hours ago, long after she'd given up hope of seeing him again, he'd called and revitalized that hope.

Now she paced up and down in her apartment, keeping a close eye on the street below. He was coming by, and they were walking to his mother's house for dinner.

Except he was fifteen minutes late. Why hadn't he texted, or called? Every time she saw him, he had his phone in his hand. Maybe he'd changed his mind and wasn't coming after all and didn't think to tell her. She should probably call his mom and cancel. She'd feel silly going to a family dinner without being accompanied by one of the family. Even with Zander at her side, it seemed like an intrusion on a family's privacy. Her boss's family at that. She was acquainted with her employer's family, but not truly friends.

She paced into the bedroom and back out again. She checked her hair in the hall mirror and smoothed the breezy pink floral fabric of her sundress. Her sweater was hanging on the back of the apartment door with her purse. She was ready to go if he ever showed up. She looked out the window just as Zander pulled up and climbed out of his truck. King jumped out right behind him.

160

She locked up and jogged down three flights of stairs and met him in the lobby. He looked amazing. His khaki chino shorts were pressed and looked incredible against the light tan of his skin. He wore a coordinating green T-shirt proclaiming him World's Best Uncle. His hair was damp, and his dark beard was neatly trimmed to look like a long five o'clock shadow. He seemed unfazed by the early evening humidity rolling in off the ocean. *Golly, he looked delicious.* Her heart frolicked in anticipation.

"Hi." She let herself through the locked inner lobby door into the foyer. *Oh my. He smells amazing.* Her skin prickled and a shiver of longing skittered down her spine. "You're late. I wondered if you'd changed your mind about going."

Gosh, she'd missed him. She told her mind to hush.

"I did text you," he said. "I had a late walk-in."

"Oh, I didn't get it." She pulled out her phone to double check. "Nothing." She showed him.

"Weird." He showed her his phone and the text he had indeed sent.

"Technology." She laughed. "Should we go?" She was feeling giddy and upbeat now that she knew she hadn't been ditched.

He held the lobby door open, and they went down the two front steps to the sidewalk. "I'll just shoot Mom a text that we're on the way. With luck it will get there before we do. A word to the wise," he paused, "I told Mom we're dating. I'm hoping it stops her matchmaking attempts."

Heather frowned. "What about Derrick? He was mad when you kissed me. He doesn't want you near me. How do we handle that?" She stopped dead on the sidewalk. "Oh man. I should have thought of this earlier. I could lose my job!"

"Relax. It'll be fine. I told Mom we were keeping it quiet for now. That we wanted to go slow and not go public until we knew if it was going to work out. I think she'll keep it under her hat."

She didn't care for the uncertainty in his voice. "Are you sure?"

"With Mom, nothing is certain. But she seemed to understand that we wanted privacy."

"I hope you're right. I don't want to lose this job."

"Honestly, I think you're worrying too much. I don't think Derrick will fire you if we're dating." The certainty in his voice was reassuring.

She resisted the urge to ask him what happened when they broke up.

Each time their shoulders bumped as they walked along the narrow sidewalk, she wanted to lean into his warmth. It wasn't that she was cold, it was more that touching him filled her with an energized contentment that she wanted, needed, more of. The contact chased away some of her fear.

She carried her purse between her hands, with her sweater hanging over top. She probably looked prissy, but it kept her hands too busy to heed the temptation to hold his hand.

She was nervous about the evening. After Zander asked her to dinner, his mother showed up in the kitchen to invite her as well. Her exact words were, "Just making sure my son didn't forget to invite you." His mom put a sarcastic emphasis on forget.

163

Heather asked the question that had been roiling in her mind all afternoon. "What do I expect tonight? I've met everyone, but I don't really know them."

"Noise. Expect a lot of noise. There will be teasing, laughter, and probably a few arguments." He chuckled. "Definitely arguments."

She bit her lip. She wasn't a huge fan of confrontation. She dealt with it fine, but she didn't like it. After the scene with Marv's pregnant wife, she wanted to keep her life calm and drama free.

"It won't be anything to worry about. We're just loud and boisterous and we fight amongst ourselves a lot. Don't let the bickering fool you. As a family, we stand together against the world."

"I'll keep that in mind." His words echoed Quinn's comment the other day.

They weren't even inside the house when the sound of raised male voices reached them. She paused at the base of the front steps.

"Go on," Zander urged. "We don't bite." He splayed his hand across the small of her back.

She swore the heat from each individual finger branded her through her dress. She stepped forward to get away from the sensation. Zander followed her up the stairs and leaned past her to open the screen door.

"We're here," he shouted toward the house from right beside her. She winced at the shard of pain piercing her eardrum.

The argument ended as if someone had flipped a switch. His mother, Beth, hurried to greet them, wiping her hands on her apron as she came. "Perfect timing. I just finished mashing the potatoes." She half turned away from them and shouted, "Derrick pull the ribs out of the oven." She threw her arms around Heather. "Welcome to the family, dear," she said loudly.

Did anyone in this family talk at a normal tone of voice? King pushed past her and wandered inside, obviously used to visiting here.

"Um. Thanks for having me over for dinner. It smells delicious." The sweet tang of barbecue sauce hung in the air along with corn on the cob, and unless she missed her guess, fresh biscuits. She couldn't remember the last time she'd had barbecue; she'd probably been a teenager. Many of her friends were chefs and it seemed that dinners with them were often fancier than they needed to be. Almost an unspoken one-upmanship contest against each other. She'd been no better than the rest, prepping intricate multi-course dinners, when a simple meal would have served as well and been more intimate and relaxing.

Beth wrapped her arms around Heather's shoulder and tugged her forward. "Don't worry about your shoes. They're fine."

"Oh no. I'll just slip them off. The heels might damage your floors." She slipped out from under Beth's arm and removed her high heeled sandals. She put on a pair of short socks and set the shoes to the side, out of the jumble of large men's footwear that littered the entryway and created a tripping hazard. She wanted to line them all up beside hers.

"Come. Come," Beth urged, "tell me all about yourself. Are you single?"

"Mom!" Zander groaned.

166

"Oh, hush. I want to know everything about your new friend."

Zander's mom was a force to be reckoned with. Heather wondered if the woman was ever denied anything she went after. Beth hustled her to the dining room table and shouted, "Come eat."

Thundering feet heralded the arrival of the rest of the family. For a moment all four sons were lined up at the side of the table. They were all different from each other but were, beyond doubt, related. Though their hair was a variety of shades, they had the same steely jaw and eyes. They looked a bit like their mother but probably resembled their father more.

Jacob was serious, as always. Derrick was scowling, and Tyson looked distracted. Zander smiled at her, and heat blossomed from her toes to the top of her head. Funny that his smile did that when none of his brothers' rare grins ever lit her insides on fire. Not that they were grinning now.

"What's with the shirt?" Derrick growled, edging past Zander with a heaping tray of ribs in his hands.

"You're not the favorite," Tyson quipped. "Everyone knows I'm the favorite uncle. I've even got the shirt to prove it." Heather stifled a laugh. Zander, Derrick, and Tyson all wore the same shirt in different colors. Jacob's said World's Best Dad while the others all said World's Best Uncle.

Ella and Lexi came in, each carrying a laden dish. "You're all my favorite." Ella's comment elicited a chorus of grumbles that made the women laugh.

The enormous dining table was set with serviceable dishes. They were mismatched in a manner that made the table feel eclectic and quirky. Heather suspected the variety of dishes was the result of years of rough and tumble boys breaking things. The drinkware ranged from ancient superhero glasses from fast food joints to those designed to mimic cut crystal. The entire table made her smile. The ribs were piled on a baking sheet and the mashed potatoes were mounded in a heavy ceramic bowl patterned with three-dimensional strawberries. Biscuits overflowed a wicker basket. There was a Royal Albert Christmas patterned gravy boat, and the iced tea was in a plastic jug. The table, like the family, was a bit chaotic and absolutely fun.

The bickering continued as everyone found their way to a seat. Mostly, it seemed good natured, but there were a few harsh verbal jabs thrown. Still, Heather recognized the love between them.

Heather sat in the chair Beth steered her toward. Ella sat on her left, Zander on her right. The table was large but crowded. Zander's knee bumped hers repeatedly. Initially, she pulled away, but it was no use. The only way to escape the delightful brushing of skin would be to leave the table entirely.

"Thank you for inviting me. This all looks amazing," Heather said.

"You are very welcome. Zander can bring you anytime. No need to wait for an invitation. There's always plenty of food to go around. Besides, you work at the inn, that practically makes you family." Beth winked at her from across the table. She suspected Zander's mother was pushing to see how serious their relationship was.

"Tyson, you should go out with Lila-Jean's daughter while she's in town next week," Beth declared giving her son a significant look.

Heather had no idea who Lila-Jean was but judging by Tyson's face the idea was not appealing in the least.

"Derrick can date her. I've been down that road. I dated Naomi in high school. Lila-Jean is lovely. Naomi, not so much. So, no, thank you."

Derrick glared at Tyson. "Don't even think of pushing that on me," he growled.

"Why is everyone bent on hooking me up?" Tyson demanded. "I'm capable of finding my own dates." He slammed a fist on the table making the glasses jump. He grabbed the dish of corn and threw a cob on his plate before shoving the dish Derrick's way. He accidentally bumped his brother's elbow as he started to take a drink of iced tea.

Liquid sloshed down Derrick's chest. The glass dropped onto his plate spraying everyone with the sugary liquid. He cussed and slammed his chair backward, tipping it over with a deafening crash. He stormed out of the room. King barked twice from under the table. The screen door slammed and seconds later a motorcycle roared to life.

When the sound faded in the distance, Beth sighed. "Pardon my sons, despite my best efforts, they sometimes behave like a bunch of barbarians."

Tyson mumbled an apology. Lexi righted Derrick's chair. Zander rose carefully to his feet and went into the kitchen. He came back with a roll of paper towel and several wet cloths.

"Don't worry about me," Heather said. "I've seen more than one fight at a dinner party." Nothing like this, but she didn't want Beth to feel worse than she already did. Both Beth and Ella looked on the verge of tears.

The mess was cleaned up and everyone patted dry. "Dig in," Beth said. "It's already getting cold." Silence reigned as bowls were passed and people began eating.

"How are you liking Half Moon Bay," Beth asked. "Are you thinking of settling down here and raising a family?"

Heather choked on her tea. "I like it here. I'm happy at the inn."

"And babies?" Beth persisted.

"Um." She floundered for an answer. "I'm young. Only thirty-four. I'm not in a big rush to reproduce. I'm not even in a serious relationship. Dating and family can wait a few years. I want to settle into my career first."

"You young girls, you're all alike. Putting off babies until your eggs dry up." She made a tsking sound.

"Mom. Stop!" Zander barked. "Heather is my guest. We're not planning on having kids. Heather's family plans are private. Give it a rest."

Beth sighed. "Fine. I'm just saying ...."

"Mom!" he warned. "Drop it."

Heather didn't know whether to laugh or cry. She was mortified. She kept telling herself she wasn't interested in him, but his dismissal of their relationship was a jab to her ego. Apparently to her heart, it didn't matter that their relationship was fake.

Holy hockey socks! She was falling for him! She nearly grabbed her heart in shock. She wanted more. They clicked and got along well. Her heart beat faster when he was near. He made her feel like she could do anything. *Jumping jackrabbits. She was in trouble.*

"Fine," Beth said. "I won't say anything else, but you kids need to know that I'm not getting any younger. I want grandkids before I'm too old to play with them. And look at sweet Ella, she's the perfect age to babysit for you."

"Mom. Stop!" Jacob growled.

"I second that." Tyson stabbed his fork into a rib.

Zander reached over and smoothed Heather's tense fingers. "Relax," he whispered, "She's harmless. You're safe from the marriage trap."

Marriage trap? Was that what he really thought of getting married? Was he that against it? Somehow, she had the impression that he wasn't opposed to marriage, just not ready yet. Crazy. She extracted her hands from his and picked up her fork and ate some potatoes and gravy.

"This is delicious, Beth." It was probably tasty, but it landed in her stomach like ball bearings.

The conversation morphed to the food and there was less chatter as everyone ate, but her mind was stuck on the idea of a relationship with Zander. She wasn't looking for a man, but somewhere deep in the back of her mind, she must have been considering him for the role. It was disappointing and a bit hurtful that he totally wrote her off as a partner. This whole fake dating and hiding even that from her bosses was a colossal mistake. She could almost count the minutes until it failed catastrophically.

Chapter 14

"That was brutal," Zander said as he walked Heather home. King trotted beside them, sniffing every post they passed. "Mom was pushy tonight. She isn't usually that bad." He paused to look at Heather. She walked along, her eyes straight to the front. She didn't seem angry, just not right somehow. She was exceptionally quiet, responding when spoken to, but not offering anything extra to the conversation.

"Mom has never made any bones about wanting grandkids, but tonight was over the top. I'm sorry."

"It's okay. I've seen her around the inn *suggesting* that Jacob and Lexi have a child. I should have expected her to comment since she thinks we're dating."

"That doesn't mean she can try and force us into a future together. I'm not ready to actually date anyone. I don't have time for that."

"But don't you think about it? Don't you think about a family of your own?" she sounded frustrated.

"I'm not ready either, but I know that a husband and family are in my not too-distant future."

Her words burrowed deep into his chest like a worm into an apple, spoiling his contentment with life. Did he want a family of his own? Could he handle taking care of his mother and siblings, and a wife and child? He would like a son, someday. One with his light brown hair. An image formed in his mind. Him, holding his son's hand as they walked down the street. Only instead of his own brown eyes, the boy had Heather's ocean-blue ones. He almost stumbled. Painful longing grew in his chest.

"Someday, I'll have a son," he said, his voice cracked with yearning. He faked a cough, so she'd think it was the cough that altered his voice, not emotion.

"I think you'll be a wonderful father. You're great with Ella and you take such good care of your siblings." She grabbed his hand and squeezed as if emphasizing her words. They kept walking, hands entwined.

"Thanks." He cleared his throat. "What about you? How many kids?"

"I think that depends on my husband. At this point, my work hours are long and sometimes erratic. I need a man who can take care of our littles when I'm at work. Someone to share the load of raising a family, of doing housework, of being a partner. He'll need to be able to help around the house, handle a full family load, and have a decent job. Kids aren't cheap and it takes a solid partnership to raise them. I'll need a man who can compromise because balancing his needs, my needs, and our children's needs is going to take a lot of work. For both of us."

Me, his mind screamed. *I could be that man. I know how to handle a family and work. I can compromise.* He clamped his lips together to keep the words in. What was he thinking? He barely knew Heather and somehow, out of the blue, he was imagining the rest of his life with her. From wedding bells, through kids and retirement, to sitting on the front porch in rocking chairs watching the world go by. *Holy crap!* The weirdest part was the idea didn't terrify him.

"I probably expect too much. But for me, marriage and children require effort and cooperation."

Finally, he managed to say, "I think it's good that you know what you want. And that you're willing to compromise with whoever you choose. That's admirable."

"Thanks. I think a relationship requires give and take from everyone involved. Raising kids won't be easy. It will take a partnership with the right man." She paused on the sidewalk beside the truck he'd left in front of her building before dinner. "My roommate is away for a couple days," she said. "Did you want to come up for a coffee or something?"

"I'd like that." He hadn't realized until she asked the question that he wasn't ready to part from her. He wanted to spend more time with her and learn more about her. Heather was by far and away, the most interesting woman he'd met in a long time. Maybe years. She'd handled his family well. She hadn't freaked out when Derrick lost his temper. She'd talked with everyone, including Ella. She could have snapped at his mother when she asked about grandchildren, but she had handled the situation with calm and aplomb. Impressive.

"Oh, what about King?" He stroked the lab's ears.

"I guess he could come," she said uncertainly. "Other people have pets."

"He'll be good, and quiet. I promise."

She led them inside and past the elevators to the stairs. They started up the staircase. It seemed narrower than a normal staircase, maybe that was an illusion caused by the fact that his heart beat louder when he climbed beside her.

He paused to tie his shoe, letting her get ahead, and giving himself a chance to breathe. It wasn't the exertion; it was her presence stealing his breath. He looked up from his shoe and realized he'd made a strategic error. Walking beside her might be difficult, but watching her long legs ahead of him on the stairs was pure torture. He jogged a couple stairs until he was beside her on the third-floor landing.

"How high are we going?" he asked.

"This is it. Were the stairs too much for you? I always take the stairs. Well, except when I have groceries." She laughed at herself.

"I'm good. But those ribs are sitting heavy right now. I ate way too much. Mom makes the best barbecue ribs." He massaged his belly as they left the stairwell.

"She does make good ribs. I could have eaten more, but I know better." She lifted the reusable grocery bag in her hand. "I can't believe she gave me leftovers. I can't wait until dinner tomorrow. Everything was amazing. That chocolate cake was divine."

"That cake was from the bakery." Zander laughed. "Mom can cook, but she can't bake."

"Oh no. I spent so much time complimenting her on it. I'm so embarrassed." Her cheeks turned the most adorable pink as she unlocked the door.

"Don't worry about it. Mom was pleased. I think she believes she's fooling us all."

"That's good. Coffee, or something else?"

He could tell she was still bothered by praising the cake, but he let the subject drop. "Have you got any beer?"

"I've got wine but not beer." She waved to the table in the small eating alcove. "Take a seat and I'll scare something up."

She moved around the kitchen with confident actions that didn't surprise him. Her light humming did. Did she hum when she worked at the inn? He was curious to find out. He forced himself to look around the apartment instead of staring at her. It was furnished simply. Wooden coffee and end tables, a bright red sofa and a couple of tan chairs. A small television and stereo. Brightly colored art prints on the walls, and books everywhere. It was homey. He wondered if the décor was hers or her roommate's.

"Want to watch something on television?" he asked when she set the wine and glasses on the table. King immediately stretched out on the throw rug.

"I'm not much for TV. How about a game of Scrabble?" she countered. "Bet I can beat you."

"You're on. I haven't lost a game of Scrabble in years." His mom taught him to play when he was a kid. They'd started with Scrabble Junior and eventually moved up to the adult game. None of his siblings had a taste for the game, but he loved playing against his mom. He even wasted time with a Scrabble app on his phone. It was the only digital game he played. He didn't play often, just a few moves now and then. Typically, he won, unless he played the computer in expert mode.

He carried the wine to the coffee table while Heather went into the bedroom and came out with the deluxe version of the game. The one with pieces that stayed in place if the board shifted. She settled cross-legged on the end of the three-seater couch and put the game on the middle cushion. "Letter closest to A goes first." She shook the purple cloth bag that held the tiles and held it out to him as he sat across from her.

He pulled an H. She pulled a V. "Your move," she declared and started arranging tiles on her rack. His letters were terrible, and he managed only eight points with sate. She played absolute using the S in his word.

"I get fifty extra points for using all my letters," she gloated. "You're going down."

They played two games and chatted, getting to know each other better. The score was close in both games.

Heather's phone rang. She glanced at it and declined the call.

"Did you need to get that?" he asked. "I don't mind."

"No. It was just my ex. He started calling last week. I have nothing to say to him and there is nothing he can say that I want to hear. The man is scum."

"Okay, if you're sure." It was odd that her ex would start calling. In her place, he'd want to know what the man wanted. He'd probably answer just for the chance to tell him off.

At the end of the second game he said, "I should go, and you better get to bed. I know you're up early to make breakfast at the inn."

She glanced at the clock. "Wow. I didn't know it was that late. You're right." They packed up the board.

"Thanks for the game. Are you sure you should drive home? We drank a bottle and a half of wine."

He was probably fine, but the idea of staying near Heather was enticing. "Maybe I should stay. I don't feel impaired, but there's no sense risking a DUI or hurting someone. Do you mind?"

"No. You can take the couch." While he took the dog outside for a moment, she found him an unused toothbrush.

"Thanks for a fabulous evening." He stood outside the bathroom, staring at Heather. No part of him wanted to walk away. He wanted, needed to say goodnight properly. He reached out and ran a finger down her cheek and neck to her shoulder. He ran both hands down her arms and clasped her hands in his.

"I should say goodnight," he whispered. He leaned toward her, watching her eyes. When he was millimeters away, they drifted shut. *Sweet heaven*. He brushed his lips over hers and let go of her hands. "Sweet dreams, sweet Heather."

"You too." Her voice was husky with unspent emotions.

He darted into the washroom and stayed there until he heard her bedroom door shut. He wanted to believe he was a gentleman, but in reality, he was a coward of the worst sort. He didn't have the guts to go for what he wanted.

What he wanted wasn't just physical, though that kiss had rocked him to his toes and sent his heart into overdrive. He was beginning to think that a relationship with Heather, a real one, might be just what he needed.

Sleep didn't come easily. He was completely caught up in thoughts of Heather. They shared a lot of opinions. They even agreed on most aspects of politics. Neither of them went to church often enough, but they both had solid faith. They meshed well together. She was invigorating and peaceful to be with. The dichotomy of his feelings was uncomfortable.

Being near Heather filled him with calm and excitement for what might come in the future. He stared up at the ceiling wondering if being her friend was going to be enough for either of them. The sun was rising before he started to drift into sleep.

Chapter 15

The overcast morning couldn't bring Heather down. The radio played softly in the inn's kitchen as she prepared for breakfast and waited for Ella to stop by on her way to school.

She hummed as she mixed cranberry bran muffins to go with the eggs benny. She was going with bacon bennies rather than ham. Breakfast was buffet style. Of course, those with special dietary needs were always welcome to order something. She slid some muffins into the oven and recalled Zander's love of her baking. It was flattering that he liked her food.

She'd had trouble dragging herself out of the apartment this morning. She wanted to kiss him awake, or better yet lay down beside him for a cuddle. Instead, she'd left him sleeping on her sofa with King beside him on the floor. The dog didn't even twitch an ear when she got up. She didn't have the heart to wake them after staying up so late last night. After too much staring, she'd left her house key on the table along with a note for Zander.

It was only six-thirty, so it was too early to expect him, but she was looking forward to seeing him. She felt ... connected to him after last night. The connection was more than she expected when she agreed to the fake date as a trial run.

She hugged herself as memories of their kiss slipped in. Holy moly. So gentle, so sweet. Brief though it was, she felt his caring in the tender press of his lips to hers. Her heart had fluttered. It was lovely, but not what she needed from him.

The goal had been to see if she was ready to trust a man again. Her first intention was helping out a friend, but she was slipping into something deeper than she anticipated and wasn't sure she objected to the change, except, of course, if it impacted her job and future plans.

Voices intruded on her thoughts. Lexi was talking to someone in the lobby. Guests didn't typically get up this early. A man's laugh barked out, breaking the near silence. Zander. She'd recognize that laugh anywhere!

Her heartbeat accelerated in anticipation. She felt like a kid on Christmas morning.

She took stock of her morning progress as she waited for him to invade her kitchen. The croissants were already cooling, and she had cookie dough in the fridge ready to hit the oven as soon as it was free. It was empowering to be on top of her work after a rough night's sleep. Knowing Zander was sleeping in the next room had made her restless and her romantic dreams about him had kept waking her.

She hummed along with a Bryan Adams tune as she worked. Sensing someone in the room, she turned and there he was. Zander leaned against the doorjamb like some kind of Greek god. Handsome, sexy, a bit scruffy and in need of a shave. He must have showered because his hair was damp. Oh, sweet heaven, he was the stuff fantasies were made of. Dragonflies danced in her belly. A tiny voice in her mind whispered, "That hunk of sweet man is mine."

"Morning." His low rumble slid across her skin like buttered whiskey leaving shivers in its wake. His smile was devastating to her equilibrium.

189

Unconsciously, she stepped toward him, needing to be closer.

"Morning." She stopped in her tracks as she struggled to get the words out past a lump of desire in her throat. A foolish grin spread across her face. "Coffee?"

"Sure. I'd like that." He ambled further into the kitchen and held out his hand. "Here's your key. Thanks for letting me sleep."

"You looked so peaceful I didn't have the heart to wake you."

He placed the key in her palm and slid his fingertips back across hers. Lightning flashed up her arm and she barely suppressed a gasp of shock. Whoa! The man packed a punch. She shoved the key in the pocket of her black work pants. She fumbled for something to keep the conversation going past her sudden attack of nerves.

He spoke before she found her voice. "I missed you this morning."

"Me too." No sense denying it.

"How long before there is something to eat?"

She laughed at the fake despair in his voice. "Just like that, you roll into my kitchen and demand food?"

"Well, I did spend the night with you last night, and usually breakfast follows a night together?"

"Whoa!"

She whirled toward the angry voice. Derrick stood in the doorway. She hadn't heard him enter.

"Something going on I should know about?" he demanded.

"No!" she blurted. "It isn't like it sounds."

"It better not be." Derrick glared at Zander. "You bothering my employee again?" His voice was more growl than words. The muscles in his jaw clenched and flexed.

Was he implying that Zander shouldn't be a pest, or that he shouldn't be spending time with Heather at all? It was hard to tell, and she couldn't force the question out.

Part of her threw out the logic that if she didn't know exactly what her boss meant, it was okay to keep seeing Zander. Her heart didn't like the deception, but she was so drawn to him she couldn't make herself ask for clarification. She let the question slide away. *Where had her normal outspokenness gone?*

"Zander walked me home after family dinner last night. He stayed for a glass of wine. We drank more than we should, and he slept on the couch. There was nothing suspect about it." Her heart thundered. She did not want Derrick to think she was doing anything with his brother. His presence was a huge reminder not to get involved with the boss's family. She needed this job! But man, under other circumstances, she'd be all over him.

Zander raised his hands in surrender. "Bro, I swear, it was all on the up and up. I'm here because she left early, and I have her house key. Plus, I'm hungry and she's the best chef in town."

She appreciated him both for backing her up and for praising her cooking. Zander Bellamie was an all-around nice guy. Well worth dating.

Fake dating, girl. It's just fake dating. Play it cool. This job is my chance to prove I'm not an idiot taken in by a handsome face. I attended that rodeo with Marv. His lying, cheating, and theft do not define me!

I've got this! I can ignore my attraction to Zander! This is all about keeping his mom off his back. Nothing more. It's fake!!

She transferred muffins from the pans to a serving platter. As much as she enjoyed Zander's company, she wasn't going to allow herself to get any closer. *Think about your career. You can't actually date Zander and take a risk of losing your heart if it goes badly. Back off, Heather. He's not for you. You need to end this fake relationship.*

But for all of her repetitive internal monolog, part of her still wondered what it would be like if they were serious about each other.

If a relationship between them was going well, there wouldn't be an issue, but if it went south? It could cause family issues. What if she fell for him and he didn't fall for her? Disaster! She'd seen enough of the Bellamie family to know that they'd stick together, and she'd be out of a job. She needed to back off and protect herself.

After Marv had done his best to blackball her in Toronto, she found it hard to trust. His betrayal went so deep she still felt the repercussions a year later. Zander seemed trustworthy but she was not going to put her entire livelihood at risk for a man, even if she was learning that some men could be trusted.

She did not need a man.

Derrick came to stand between her and Zander.

"Are you sure he isn't being a pest?" He frowned at his brother.

She'd been so lost in her thoughts it took a minute to process his question. "I'm sure." She flashed Derrick her best smile. "Your brother is a decent man and nothing but respectful. I'm new to town and he's been a good friend."

Beyond Derrick, she saw Zander's flinch at the word friend. Was he thinking they were more? He better not be. Despite their kiss last night, she was not going there. Though she did want to taste him again. Frustrated by her waffling thoughts and emotions, she focused her attention on cooking.

Derrick grumbled under his breath and left the kitchen. She'd dodged a bullet there.

"May I please have a muffin?" Zander asked apologetically.

"Help yourself."

He carefully peeled away the paper, broke off the bottom and started eating it.

"Don't most people eat the top first?" she teased, feeling safer now that Derrick was gone.

"The top, while it is still crispy, is the best part. I eat it last." He devoured another bite. "This is amazing. It's so rich and moist it doesn't even need butter. That's impressive for a bran muffin. They always need butter."

"Thank you. It's a modification of my grandmother's recipe."

"Well, kudos to you and your grandmother." He paused and a smile lit his eyes. "The inn could totally sell these at the Canada Day, Independence Day celebration! We'd make a ton of money for charity."

"I didn't realize the long weekend celebration was a charity event." She took the rest of the bacon out before it got too crispy. Unable to resist, she nibbled one of the cooler pieces. Man, she loved bacon.

"Traditionally, it is for charity. This is the seventy-fifth anniversary of the event. Every year the money raised goes to a different charity. Once, about a decade ago, we used the funds to rebuild a house that burned down. The family had no insurance. I think the mayor's office keeps a list of applicants."

"I could make cupcakes or muffins for charity. And cookies, if Derrick wanted me to." She poured Zander a coffee and placed it on the small staff table in the corner before returning her attention to making bennies now that the bacon was ready.

Half an hour later, he was still in her kitchen, drinking coffee and watching her cook. "I probably should consider going to work." He picked up his coffee. It didn't look like he had any intention of moving.

"You better eat first." She'd moved on to making more bennies to replace what had been eaten. The inn wasn't huge, but apparently, the guests were ravenous today.

She filled a plate with food and set it in front of him. She dropped into a chair beside him and asked, "Where is the festival held?"

"I think the plan is to host the event here at the inn. We, and by that, I mean Jacob, has a ton of land, right on the coast. It's the perfect spot for a clam bake and chowder party. There's always a chowder cookoff and a bonfire."

"Can I enter the cookoff?"

Zander's laugh elicited her own. "I don't think that would be fair. Of course, if you wanted to cook just for me, I'm game. I love a good chowder or bouillabaisse, or an old-fashioned fish boil."

"I suppose you want that with garlic-cheddar biscuits, and deep-dish apple pie and ice cream?" She poured herself a coffee from the carafe on the table and offered him a refill. He waved it away as he ate.

"Well, apple pie is traditional on Independence Day. After all, what's more American than apple pie?"

"I have no idea. I'm Canadian. We typically have strawberry shortcake on Canada Day. But, since we're celebrating both, we can eat both. I'll add them to the weekend's menu."

"You're making me hungry," he declared licking the last of the hollandaise sauce off his fork. His phone chimed and he pulled it out and texted something before sliding it back in his pocket.

"How can you even think about more food? You just ate two bennies, extra bacon, hashbrowns, and a side of fruit salad."

"And a muffin." His grin was irrepressible. "I smell cookies too. If I asked really nicely, could I get cookies to go, for my coffee break?"

Ella raced into the run to hug her uncle. "Uncle Zander, can you give me a ride to school?"

"Sure, if it's okay with your dad."

"It's okay with me," Lexi said, coming into the room right after Ella. "And no, you can't get cookies to go. You're eating us out of house and home." Heather knew that Lexi was hoping Jacob would propose. They both treated Ella like they were engaged already.

In the short time Lexi had been around, mere months, she and Zander had always gotten along, teasing one another with impunity.

"Grinch." He mock pouted.

Lexi patted him on the shoulder. "Sorry, dude. It's only June. The Grinch is a Christmas thing." She rummaged around in the pantry and pulled out a small paper lunch bag. She slipped a few of yesterday's leftover cookies into it and sat it in front of him. "Don't forget the bag is compostable. Thanks for driving Ella to school. You better get going, or you'll both be late." Cookie in hand, Lexi strolled out of the kitchen without a backward glance.

"You ready munchkin?" Zander asked.

The young teen sighed. "Yeah."

"Come on. It can't be that bad. You'll have new friends before you know it."

"Here's your lunch." Heather passed over another bag. She'd taken to making Ella's school lunches knowing she hated to do it herself. It was fun to see what gained compliments and what came back uneaten. It also helped her hone down what teens liked to eat, providing valuable knowledge for her future menus.

"Thanks. Your lunches are the best."

Zander looked entirely too content and handsome as he led his niece out of the kitchen. Standing there, watching them go, she wished she was going with them. At the last second, he turned and flashed her a heart stopping wink.

"Down girl," she muttered to herself as she made her way into the dining room to check on diners and the buffet. He's too busy for an actual relationship and he's the boss's brother. You aren't interested in him. She sighed. Get your career together, Heather. Then you can find a life partner. Zander Bellamie is not the man for you.

But a girl could dream. Right?

And, man-oh-man, was she dreaming.

Twenty minutes later he texted her. "Want to go out for lunch tomorrow?"

Oh no! She was fast losing the ability to see their fake dates as pretend. They were becoming too real.

Still, her naughty fingers typed out, "Sure. See you at eleven."

Chapter 16

"Where are we going?" Heather asked as they walked along the beach holding hands. There were just enough people around she suggested holding hands to make it look like they were closer than they were. She told herself it was for appearances, not because she enjoyed his touch. King raced ahead chasing the tennis ball Zander had thrown.

"For an early lunch." He was quiet for a minute. "I keep wondering why you agreed to be my fake girlfriend. When I suggested it, you asked what was in it for you. Later, you agreed. Now, I have to admit to being curious."

"Honestly? Marv screwed me up pretty good. I have trust issues. Watching Jacob and Lexi makes me wonder what it would be like to care for and trust a man." She sucked in a breath. "Zander, I have to admit, I'm using you to rebuild my broken trust. Everyone who knows you likes you. I think that makes you trustworthy. You're my practice. Kind of like a rebound guy." *Whew! Enough soul baring for one day.*

He winced.

Interesting.

"Good to know. I appreciate you agreeing. Maybe you'll learn to trust again, and I can get some peace. Old ladies are coming out of the woodwork to flaunt their eligible daughters." He shuddered.

King raced back and dropped the tennis ball at their feet. Zander didn't seem to notice so she picked it up and threw it as far down the beach as she could. She laughed as he yipped once and raced after it. She still wasn't comfortable around the black lab, but she was doing better. Unless she and Zander went out to eat, the dog was always around. This was their official fifth date, and she was warming up to the gentle giant. His jumbo enthusiasm still made her nervous and other dogs might always freak her out, especially the small yappy ones.

Nerves clenched in Heather's stomach. She'd been right. This was a mistake. She was enjoying Zander's company. Lying to his family bothered her conscience.

Despite all that, it was nice to 'date' without pressure. Zander seemed to be financially solvent, and they shared expenses when they went out together. They often walked along the beach. It beat sitting at home alone or hiding in the public library when Quinn had Duke at the apartment. It was great, but his brothers didn't know they were dating. Derrick was sure to be upset.

They strolled toward the Crab Shack for an early lunch. "Do you think Derrick would let me use the garden to grow tea ingredients?"

"How would I know? There's a ton of unused space. Why don't you ask him? Or ask Jacob. As manager Derrick might defer to Jacob as landowner. I can't imagine it would be a problem. If you're going to try and sell the teas, you better research the public health requirements first."

"The inn's kitchen is food certified. I will have to find a place to dry the herbs." She sighed. There was so much to consider and so much she wanted to do. Working in the inn's kitchen was so much more satisfying than she thought it might be. It was an entirely different atmosphere than a city kitchen. She adored the Bellamie family and their guests. Having total control over the menu was invigorating and satisfying. She could be happy there, career-wise, if she had a way to create the tea blends she dreamed of. Maybe she could work out a tea partnership with the inn.

"I guess I'll come up with a plan about my tea," she said. "I'll ask for a meeting with them both and see what they say." She paused. "After the July long weekend. I have enough on my plate for that already. No pun intended."

"I think that's a great plan."

"How's clinic life? How's that fox?" she asked, not wanting to focus the entire conversation on herself.

"Little Red is amazing." His enthusiasm was inspiring. "She whelped yesterday. Four perfect kits. She hates her cast, but since the kits arrived, she's not chewing it so much. I've started looking for a veterinarian who might want to hire on. Tourist season is ramping up and I'm getting busier. I find that

I want more time away from the office." He smiled at her making her heart sing.

"Are you thinking you'll get a partner?"

"I was actually thinking more like becoming a teaching hospital with a focus on recent grads. They'd be paid a good wage and could upgrade their skills until they felt ready to branch out on their own. I'm not ruling out a partner, but I'd like to give new grads a hand up in their careers, like the one I got fresh out of uni."

"Very nice." And so perfectly typical Zander. Always helping someone else out. She wondered if his idea would free up more time or take more. They barely found time to 'date' as it was. He was always running off to fix something. Last night, he'd cancelled because Ella needed help with her science project.

It wasn't the last-minute cancellation that bothered her, it was that he didn't invite Heather to join them. There was a lot of science in cooking, and she might have been able to help. She also knew that Ella had procrastinated starting the project until the last minute. At the same time, it was probably best if they didn't spend too much time together around the inn and jeopardize her job.

"There she is," Zander declared, drawing Heather's attention from her self-pity and inner griping. "The Crab Shack."

Heather looked up at the building in the distance. She'd never walked this far south on the beach. The crab shack did indeed look like a shack. It sat high up on stilts with a deck surrounding it that ran out, down some steps, to a long dock. The building and deck looked weathered and almost as if they would fall down any minute.

"Are you sure it's safe to eat here?" she asked doubtfully.

Zander chuckled. "Absolutely. It's only six years old and it is rock solid. Jeremy built it to look old. As they climbed the steps, she noticed a wheelchair ramp running up the back from a paved parking lot. Okay, maybe it wasn't as bad as it appeared. The steps were solid, and the railings were wrought iron and rust free.

"You'll like Jer," Zander said. "He used to cook somewhere in New York. I think he was even on *Iron Chef* once."

She stopped at the top of the stairs and grabbed his arm. "Are you telling me that Jeremy Osten lives in Half Moon Bay? Tell me you aren't pulling my leg!"

"Ya, that's him. Why the excitement?"

"He's only my favorite chef of all time." She did a happy dance. "I can't believe I get to meet him. Oh, I hope he's here." She giggled. "Best day ever. Hurry." She dragged him toward the door.

"Slow down." He laughed. "King, go under the deck and stay." The dog whined.

"I swear he understands English," she said as the dog loped back down the stairs.

"I've had dogs my whole life. He's the best behaved of all of them. He was training to be a bomb dog but failed out. He doesn't have a suspicious nature. He loves everyone. But he listens well. Every command I give him has been reinforced with treats and pats. We come here a lot. He knows the routine."

They went inside. The décor was pure beach cliché with fishing nets, anchors, lobster pots and lanterns hung everywhere. A glass fronted bookcase held a selection of marine textbooks and novels, including at least five copies of *Moby Dick*, none of them the same. It was adorable. The air was heavy with spices and unless she missed her guess, fresh fish stew.

"Jer, you here?" Zander called as they wandered between empty tables toward the bar that ran along the back of the room.

"Right out," someone, probably Jer, called from the kitchen.

Twenty seconds later, before she fully had her bearings, Jeremy Osten strolled out of the kitchen, two big baskets in his hands. He set the dishes of peanuts and pretzels on the bar and reached out to shake Zander's hand.

"Dude, how are you?" Jeremy grinned. He didn't wait for an answer, he turned to Heather and smiled a ten-thousand-megawatt smile. "And who is your lovely friend?"

She stepped forward and thrust her hand at him. "Heather Olsen. I'm honored to meet you, Mr. Osten."

"Lovely to meet you. Call me Jer or Jeremy." He kept smiling and without breaking his gaze said, "Dude, you know I'm not open for another half hour. But I'll forgive you for bringing me this glorious creature." He winked.

"Can I see your kitchen? Can we talk cooking?" she blurted.

Jeremy laughed. "Absolutely. This one's a charmer." He led her behind the bar into the kitchen leaving Zander behind.

"What about me?" Zander asked, a laugh in his voice. "She's my date."

"What about you?" Jer quipped. "Heather are you a chef or just a fan?" he asked.

"Both. I loved you on *Iron Chef*. I'm the chef at the Inn on Half Moon Bay. Zander's brother owns it. I was blessed that they hired me." She looked around at all the gleaming stainless-steel surfaces. "Wow. This is amazing. So different from the outside. What brought you to Half Moon Bay?"

"I'm glad you like it. I got tired of the rat race. I wanted some peace and quiet. I sold my chain of restaurants and here I am."

"You retired?"

"Not really, no. I just wanted to have more free time. I love the ocean. I came here on vacation and never left. I'm ready for a family and couldn't do that and run eight restaurants at the same time. What can I cook for you? Or what can we cook together?" He winked again, this time more seriously.

She laughed. "I'm with Zander," she said. "But I'd love to cook with you."

"Lucky dude. My loss. But if you ever change your mind and want a real man, you know where to find me." His voice was full of teasing.

Zander groaned. "Dude."

Jer totally ignored her *boyfriend*. "Okay then, what shall we cook?"

"Oh, do you have a signature dish? Zander said the salmon with macadamia nuts and fried shallots was to die for. Can we make that?"

"As it happens that is my signature dish for The Shack. It's a cold dish, but I'm game. Let's turn up the heat in this kitchen." He winked again.

Wow. The guy was all flirt, but in a fun, friendly way. Once upon a time it might have been entertaining to date him, today he held absolutely no appeal beyond his cooking skills. In comparison to Zander, he came up short.

"I'm honored that you'll cook with me." She grinned. She was more than a little star-struck and showing her fangirl and didn't care in the least. She totally needed his autograph. "Dang. If I'd known I was going to meet you, I would have brought your book. You could have autographed it."

"Swing by anytime. Always happy to sign for a fan."

"Jer ...." Zander's voice held a light warning.

"Zander can be our gopher since he can't cook," Jeremy quipped in response. "There's a pen and paper in the office," he jabbed toward the corner with his thumb. "Can you grab them, Zander? I'm sure your lovely date will want to copy the recipe."

Zander wandered toward the office.

"You'd let me do that?" she gushed.

"Under the condition that you never share it, use it only for personal use, and if you plan to serve it publicly, you must modify it into something entirely your own. I don't give out my secrets lightly."

"Then why are you sharing?" She didn't want to seem ungrateful, but it seemed odd that he'd eagerly share his signature dish. Not that she couldn't figure it out with enough practice.

Jeremy leaned close and whispered, "Because it bugs the heck out of Zander that we're working together." He laughed.

"Of course, it doesn't bother him. We're only fake dating to keep the old ladies from setting him up." She confided for his ears only.

"Heather, you may be beautiful, but if you can't see that Bellamie can't keep his eyes off you, you're blind." He clapped his hands together then rubbed them briskly. "Wash up and we'll get started."

She stared at Zander as he came out of the office. Surely Jeremy was wrong. Wasn't he? She smiled and winked at Zander. He winked back, his smile growing a mile wide.

Oh oh. Maybe he did like her. Was that a good thing or not?

Her mind screamed, "No, you don't want him to fall for you."

Her heart whispered, "It's the best thing ever."

Chapter 17

Zander stomped toward Heather and Jeremy. What was Osten doing? What kind of person hit on someone else's girl? He'd shared more than a few beers with the man. He considered them friends. He banked his ire and handed Heather the pen and paper.

"What can I do?" He asked, controlling the urge to throw his arm around Heather to lay claim. The primitive urge shocked him. "I'm pretty good in the kitchen. Mom taught me a thing or two. She wanted us all to learn to cook. I failed as a kid, but living alone forces you to figure things out."

"I didn't know you could cook." Heather gave him a giant smile.

"Next date, you're cooking for me," she declared.

A buzzer sounded. "That'll be my fish order. Bellamie, you want to get that. Check the boxes off the inventory for me? If I go, this dish will be ruined."

He narrowed his eyes at Jer's smirk. The man was pushing his limits. Normally, he'd help without caring, today, he didn't want to leave Heather in Jer's clutches. "Sure. No problem," he ground out through gritted teeth.

He'd noticed the shipping receiving door on the far side of the kitchen near the office. He went over and opened it.

"Hey, where's Jer?" the driver said in greeting.

"Busy giving a cooking lesson," Zander growled. "What's the routine?"

"I bring 'em in. You check 'em off." He passed over a clipboard with a shipping slip on it.

Twenty tubs of fresh ice-packed fish, six boxes of frozen items, and eight crates of live crab and lobster later. Zander was more than glad to see the last of the driver. He returned the driver's salute and began transferring stock to the right locations. One by one, Zander carried the perishables into the walk-in fridge and toted the frozen items to the adjacent freezer. No way on earth was he handling the tubs of live stuff. He made his way back to the counter, trying not to be annoyed.

"What's cookin', good lookin'?" he asked Heather.

"We've got a crab quiche in the oven and we're working on salmon with macadamia nuts and fried shallots. I'm learning so much," she gushed. "Jer is amazing."

She smiled, genuinely happy that she was enjoying herself. Deep inside, jealousy reared its ugly head. He leaned against the counter feigning calm. "That's fabulous." He wished he were anywhere but here. "I can't wait to taste it. She's a pretty talented chef, isn't she?"

He wanted to smack his forehead. Why was he pointing out her good qualities? He didn't want Jer to fall for Heather. She was his date ... his fake date.

"She sure is. Did you know we trained at the same school a couple of years apart? How cool is that?"

He bit down so hard his teeth hurt and his head started to ache. "Cool."

His phone chimed. He ignored it. Two minutes later it chimed again. And again.

"Aren't you going to get that?" Heather asked shock evident in her voice. "It might be important." *Did she just put subtle emphasis on important?*

"It could be your family," she added.

Yup, that was a shot.

"You better check." She turned her attention back to Jeremy.

He pulled out his phone. It was his answering service. It was a bit old-school, but he used a professional service to answer the office phone when the office was unoccupied. It gave his patients a sense of calm to know he'd be in touch right away.

He texted back and forth with the service before concluding that there was a real emergency not just a nervous pet parent. Frustration rose in his chest. "I have to go. Unfortunately, this won't wait."

"Oh no," Heather said. He was impressed that she managed to sound upset. He was surprised she could tear her attention from her favorite chef. His mind sneered favorite.

"No worries. You stay here. Finish cooking. Are you okay to walk home alone?"

"I can give her a drive once my sous chef arrives," Jer volunteered.

Jealousy battled relief. "That'd be great." His phone chimed again, and he barely resisted the urge to throw it at the wall. He glanced at it. "That's my cab." He pulled Heather into his arms and brushed a kiss across her brow. "Later, sweetheart," he murmured into her silky hair. "I'll call you when I'm finished. We can pick up this date later."

He clapped Jer on the back. "Take care of my girlfriend." Why in the world had he said that? They weren't dating. They were faking. Too late now.

Working with Jeremy Osten was a total fangirl moment. Not only was he talented, but he was also kind and funny. All the same, he held no real appeal for her. They got along famously, but half of her mind was fretting about what called Zander away. Hopefully it wasn't anything too serious. It sounded like an emergency. She hoped everything was okay with his family.

Two hours later The Crab Shack was full of happy patrons and Jeremy's staff was buzzing around the kitchen. She was sitting in the office with Jer discussing recipes and people they both knew. Zander hadn't returned and she knew it was time to go.

"Thanks so much for teaching me your recipe. I'm honored that you shared it. And thanks for feeding me. I guess Zander's emergency was serious since he's not back. I'll head out now. The walk home isn't far." She stood and offered her hand. "It was a pleasure to get to know you."

"Come back anytime, and if you ever need a job, I'll find a place for you." He gave her hand a squeeze. "You should know that your ex's new place is failing badly. He can cook, but he has no management skills and can't keep staff."

She fought back a vindictive grin. "I don't wish ill on him, but that does make me happy. Thanks for telling me. Swing by the inn, and I'll fix you something special to eat. My treat."

"I'll do that."

He walked her outside and down the stairs. King exploded out of the deck shade toward her. She backed away from his exuberance. "Yikes."

"Hey, King." Jeremy patted the dog on the head. "You watching him?"

"No! I can't believe Zander left him behind." She backed away again and pointed under the deck. "King, stay." The dog tipped his head sideways and grinned at her. "Sit," she commanded. The beast just stood there panting and smiling.

"King, go lay down," Jeremy said. The dog ignored him too.

"What do I do now?"

"Just go. Maybe he'll stay here and wait for Zander. If not, it's a small town and he'll be easy to find. I'm sure most of Half Moon Bay will recognize the beast. Certainly, anyone with a pet will."

"Thanks again."

Jeremy loped back up the stairs with a wave, and she started home. She'd only taken three steps when King was beside. "Stupid animal," she grumbled. "Go lay down."

King yipped once and kept walking.

"What am I supposed to do with you? I don't even like you." Well, he seemed okay, but he was large and scary. Since the wild cat episode, animals had never been her thing. What if he went crazy? Zander wasn't here to control him, and he didn't listen to her. She tried over and over to get the dog to go back to The Crab Shack.

"That's it. I give up. I guess I'll let you walk me home." Not that she had any other choice.

The emergency was a cat who had been attacked by a wild cat. Sewing him up took nearly three hours. It was a wonder the domestic animal survived at all. Something must have interrupted the fight.

Giving the cat 160 stitches after ensuring there was no other major damage might have gone faster if thoughts of Heather and Jeremy hadn't distracted him. He thought it would be a treat for her to meet a famous chef. Boy, was he right. Too right. She was probably still there, soaking up Jer's sexy charm.

He wrapped everything up and once the animal was settled, he gave his assistant instructions on what to watch for. In the past, he'd simply stayed at the clinic with his animals. Since he started 'dating'

Heather, he'd hired a young girl who was in town for the summer. She was a veterinary tech student and happy to take part-time, casual work. He still needed more staff, but he'd made a start.

He scrubbed up and headed upstairs for something to eat. He'd skipped breakfast and his lunch had been cancelled. He was ravenous. He left the exam room and entered the clinic lobby. A soft whisper of sound caught his attention.

"Zander. Are you okay?" Heather asked. "You're as white as a ghost. Oh, I bet you didn't eat anything. Come. Let me feed you something."

"Why are you here? Why aren't you with Jeremy?" He was too tired to filter his words.

She smiled. "Because I was on a date with you? Because he has customers and a restaurant to run. Or, because you forgot your dog when you rushed away. Choose the one that suits you best," she teased.

King wandered over and leaned into his legs.

"Holy crap." He patted his pet. "I'm sorry boy." Wait. She was afraid of King. "You brought him home?"

"Well, more like when I started home, he followed me. I couldn't really leave him behind, so we walked to my place, and got my car." She made a ta-da gesture. "And here we are. How is the animal you had to help?"

"She'll be fine," he said. "I have my tech watching her. How did you get in?"

"I tried the door. It was open." She shrugged. "Since I was here already, I thought I'd wait until you finished and see if you wanted to continue our date. If you're not too busy."

"Definitely not too busy." Seeing her had revived his flagging energy. If he ate something, he'd be right as rain. "Thanks for coming and thanks for bringing my dog home."

"You're welcome."

"I need to eat. Where would you like to go?" he asked.

"How about I cook for you? It is what I do." She chuckled.

"I'd like that. My apartment is upstairs. Let's go up and see what there is to cook. We can get the market to deliver anything else you need." She'd cooked for him on one of their dates, and he'd eaten at the inn several times. He was excited to have her cook jut for him again. More importantly, he was relieved that she hadn't been taken in by Jer's charms. She followed him upstairs, King hot on their heels.

"He's a good dog," she said. "Once I was certain I couldn't get rid of him and I had to take him, he just followed along. He even hopped into the back seat of my car without me forcing him too. He's much more calm than other dogs."

He unlocked the door to his apartment and led her inside.

"Oh, this is nice." Heather said. She looked around the open concept space. "It's so bright and I love the leather furniture. I never would have guessed this was up here. It's so spacious. I love the oak cupboards. Do you like living right on top of the office?"

He smiled at the run-on words. She must be nervous.

"I never really thought about it, it's handy to be this close when I have overnight patients. The yard is great in summer too." He gestured to the window that overlooked the spacious backyard. "The last vet was a family man."

She looked out the window. "There are even flower beds and a garden." She pivoted to mock glare at him. "But they're empty. Didn't you plant anything?" she teased.

"When do I have time to garden? Between pitching in at the inn, work, family, dating, I don't have time for anything else."

A frown darkened her eyes. He was reminded of the shadows he used to see in her eyes, and realized that over the last week or so, he'd seen those shadows less and less. Maybe she was coming to terms with whatever put them there. Maybe being with him helped. "Of course," he added, "I'm rather enjoying the dating part. You're good company."

He pulled her into his arms with a sigh of relief. He'd missed her and had fretted about her leaving him for Jer.

Shock rocketed through him like a strike of lightning.

Dang it. He was falling for her. He looked her straight in the eye and said, "I missed you, and now I have to kiss you." He waited several seconds, giving her time to object. Kissing her felt right, like what he needed. What did she need?

"Heather, may I kiss you?"

Her eyes widened in shock. Her pupils dilated and she nibbled her lip before nodding.

He studied her expression, looking for the slightest bit of hesitation. He'd jumped the gun when he kissed her in the kitchen, and again in her apartment. He wasn't about to make that mistake again. He must have hesitated too long because she lifted her face toward him.

"Stop thinking," she whispered against his lips.

Electricity shot down his spine. Jolting him to life. Wow! His entire body woke. She leaned into him, tangling her fingers in his hair, and tugging him closer as they kissed. He could do this all day. She felt like coming home.

She's not yours. You have no right.

Slowly, he backed away and fumbled for what to say.

"We shouldn't be kissing," she blurted, stealing his thoughts and the words he couldn't find. "I don't know why I did that! We're not dating."

Slowly, he nodded his agreement. "But it was nice," he said.

She frowned and slapped his arm. "It was better than nice, you jerk."

She had no idea how much better than nice it was. It was heart stealing, soul mending, nice. It was perfect. Maybe they should take this fake relationship into the real zone. Except she didn't want real. She was only doing this for him. He was her rebound guy.

He got what he asked for ... what if it wasn't enough?

He recalled the time he'd asked his mother for a chocolate cake for his birthday. He was sure she believed he meant to share it. He didn't. He ate the entire thing by himself and suffered the consequences later. To this day, he heard her quiet voice saying, "Be careful what you wish for. Sometimes you don't want what you think you want." Lesson learned.

The incident was a perfect reflection of this fake relationship. He got what he wanted and now he wanted more and didn't know how to ask for it.

Chapter 18

Today would be their seventeenth fake date. Not that she was counting.

Heather was waiting inside the lobby of her building when a lovely, bright green Camaro pulled up. She hurried out immediately when Zander exited the vehicle.

"Wow. Nice car." She stroked her hand down the fender. "What happened to your truck?" Like the car, his truck was top of the line, but was perfect for hauling his supplies. He'd raved about that feature more than once.

"I don't use Betsy very often," he confessed with a self-deprecating grin. "She's for long hauls. And dates." He winked.

"Is this a date?" she teased, wishing it were.

"Danged if I know." He scraped a hand through his hair, disturbing its perfect style. "Honestly, if the truth were told, and if I wasn't protecting myself, or worried about potential fallout hurting your employment with my brother ..." His pause was agonizingly long. His face ran through several different expressions and stopped on a hesitant grin. "Yeah, it's a date. A real date. Nothing fake about it."

She felt a happy grin growing. Then, he didn't shut up.

"I like you. A lot. Probably too much. I'm busy. I have so much on my plate that I don't have time for everything. Particularly not dating. I've got staff to train, animals to look after, wild critters to rehab, a family to supervise. Dating takes too much time."

"Are you done?" she asked in a huff. "I get it. I'm not worth dating time. Can we just drop it?" Hurt squeezed her chest until she could barely draw a breath. Tears brimmed in her eyes. Thankfully, her sunglasses hid them. "You know what? On second thought, I think this whole fake dating thing isn't working for me. Thanks for the fun times we had, but I think I'm done. Later, Zander." She could barely force the words out past the lump in her throat. She gave him a careless finger waggle and turned to go back inside.

She'd only gone two steps when he called out, "Wait!" The crack in his voice stopped her cold. She froze but didn't turn back toward him.

"Heather. I didn't mean that the way it sounded. I'm trying to be honest with you," he sighed.

"Honestly is always the best policy," she quipped trying to sound unaffected by this ridiculously painful conversation. She curled her toes in her sandals to keep from turning to face him.

"If I'm honest," he went on. "I don't know what the heck I want. I don't have enough hours in the day, but I'm damned if I can stay away from you. You draw me like a tick to a dog."

She whirled round to glare. "Now I'm a tick?" The man had gall, that's for sure.

"No." He scraped a hand over his face. "I'm messing this up." He took three audible breaths. "Heather, I like you. A lot."

"Yeah, you said that." She couldn't contain the snarky response.

He hurried around the car and gripped her hands. "I think we should stop fake dating."

"Isn't that what I just said?" Her heart clenched and for a moment, she was sure she could feel it bleeding into her chest, filling her lungs, stealing her breath. Could you die from a broken heart?

"No!" He shouted. "I mean, you did say that, but that's not what I meant." He muttered low under his breath. "I'm messing this up."

"Ya think?" As painful as this conversation was, there was something endearing about his inability to get his words together.

"Heather, we've been on a lot of fake dates now. Something isn't working. I don't want to fake date you." He held up a hand to stop her from interrupting. "I want to for-real date you." He winced again and stepped toward her. "No lies. No subterfuge. Just two adults spending time together to see where it goes." He squeezed her hands in his. "Heather Olsen, would you go steady with me?"

She was torn between laughing at the childish question and throwing her arms around him in joy.

"Conditionally, yes." She raised a finger. "First, your brother must agree that it is okay and that I won't lose my job if we break up." He nodded so she went on. "Second, you have to know that nothing will stop me from building the career I want. I will own a bakery someday. I love cooking, but my passion is teas and baking. You're addicted to my cupcakes and muffins, you know how talented I am. Third, you tell your mother that we were faking and that we are now actually dating."

"Yes, to all of that." He said, drawing her into a hug. "Is that it?"

"Probably not. I'm sure there is something I'm forgetting."

"Again," he said seriously. "I accept your conditions, and those that come. But in exchange, you have to try not to compare me to your ex."

"Done," she agreed happily.

"Heather Olsen, can I take you out for dinner? An official date. My treat."

"Yes, you may." She was halfway into the car when another condition popped into her mind. "One more condition."

"Okay," he said, caution squelched his previous happy tone.

"When that danged phone rings or bings, if it isn't an emergency, you let it go. You let whoever is on the other end know that you're busy and will get back to them. I deserve to be the center of your attention." It was a hard stance. One that was likely to end their newfound agreement, but it meant a lot to her. After he dumped her at The Crab Shack, she understood that she would always come second, never first. If it stayed that way, she wasn't interested in going forward.

She fully understood animal emergencies, and actual family emergencies. But to rush off because his mother needed baking soda was ridiculous.

"I can promise you that I'll try." He smiled hopefully.

She closed her eyes and counted to ten. Was that good enough? "You get three warnings. Three screwups and we're done. Got it?"

He winced. "I can live with that. I swear," he crossed his heart and offered his pinky finger over the car, "I swear I'll do my best to put you first."

"Except in actual emergencies. And Lexi needing ice cream is not an emergency. Nor is Ella's need for a ride to her friend's house. Nor is your mother needing her garden watered." She listed the three most irksome interruptions she had endured.

His smile went straight to her toes. "It's hard to deny them. They're my family and my responsibility."

"With the exception of Ella, who has other uncles and parents to do her bidding, they're all adults capable of solving their own problems and running their own lives," Heather reminded him.

"True."

She waited because his expression said he was mulling the idea over.

"I agree to decline all non-emergencies," he said. "I made reservations. Shall we go before we lose them?"

"Thank you." She slid in and buckled her seatbelt. "Yes, please. I'm hungry. Where are we headed?" she asked.

"You have to wait and see." He smirked. He drove the short distance to town and pulled into the grocery store parking lot.

"Really?" She raised one eyebrow.

He laughed. "Don't be silly." He held out a scarf. "Blindfold yourself. I want this to be a surprise."

She squinted at him. "This is pretty odd for a fake date."

"Okay, I had a plan to take you to dinner and ask if we could stop faking. I still have a plan. Cover your eyes and play along. I promise not to hurt you."

"Okay?" She bound her eyes with the silk scarf and wondered what a bachelor was doing with a wild rose print scarf. Funny, it exactly matched the pink in her dress and in her favorite sweater. The silk was cool and slippery as it whispered against her skin. It reminded her of his fingers on her face.

"I love that you're being a good sport."

Her heart tripped into overtime when he said love. *Calm down. He doesn't mean you. You and your attitude are two different things.* "I try to be accommodating." She straightened the scarf. "Okay. Ready."

The car backed up, turned, and moved forward. She tried to listen for sounds that might give her a clue where they were headed. They turned right. Left. Right again. They went straight for several minutes and took a few more turns. He flipped on the radio, distracting her from thinking about their route. For a long time, they didn't change directions except for small swerves.

"We're on the highway," she exclaimed.

"Can you see?" She heard the frown in his voice. Interesting how she could hear a facial expression when she was without her vision.

"No, but we haven't turned for several minutes. That means highway. Where are we going?" She could have felt nervous. It was a sign of how much she cared for him that she didn't feel unsafe, only confident that she'd be fine.

"Patience, Heather. All in good time."

Time lost all meaning as they drove. It might have been five minutes, or twenty. He flipped between radio stations, so she couldn't use the number of songs to track time. He was devious in the extreme.

Finally, they slowed and stopped.

"Are we there? Can I look?" She wiggled in excitement.

"Soon. Hang tight. I'll come around and get you."

His door opened and closed. Hers opened. She stepped out and his hand caressed her shoulder and slid down to clasp her hand. "Smooth walking for a minute."

Her heels tapped on what sounded like cement. Maybe concrete. "Texture change," he warned, and her heels sank into soft ground. Birds twittered and a breeze ruffled her hair.

"Sit here," he said quietly as he guided her hand to a chair. She followed the wooden back's curve until she located the seat. Anticipation built as she sat. They were eating outside. She listened hard. There were no sounds of silverware or dishes. No voices. No laughter.

Interesting. Probably not a restaurant considering the quiet and the soft ground.

"Sit tight. I'll be right back."

She listened hard and heard a soft snick sound. It was familiar but she couldn't place it. A rustle came next, then a loud pop. Champagne? "Zander?"

"Almost ready." He sounded very pleased with himself.

She felt rather than heard him step close to her. His sexy scent tickled her nose and her hands itched to reach out to him. She clenched her fists to keep them still.

"Okay. You can peek." His voice was right beside her ear.

She fumbled with the tight knot she'd tied.

"Let me help." His fingers nudged hers and she dropped her hands lest she clasp his. "Open your eyes," he whispered once the silk dropped away.

She peeked, blinked, and looked again. "Oh my gosh," she exclaimed. Though dusk was a long way off, fairy lights hung from every tree. A trio of candles in jars sat at the edge of a table covered in a white cloth.

The table was set with white dishes, crystal glasses, and shining silverware.

"Champagne?" He held up a bottle.

She swallowed hard. Where had this romantic man come from? "Yes, please." Her voice cracked. Her mouth was dry. Bliss and uncertainty skittered across her heart.

He poured and placed the champagne bottle in a long-legged wine chiller. A sea green vase on a side table held a giant bouquet of flowers. Roses nestled alongside daisies, greens, and carnations. "It's lovely," she managed to squeak out.

Way too much for a fake date. He had planned to take this a step further before their confrontation earlier! She almost giggled. He sat across from her.

Reality dawned. "This is your yard," she exclaimed. "I recognize the gardens, though they look different from down here."

"Yes. It is." Soft instrumental music started playing from speakers she couldn't locate. Zander nodded and on a whisper of sound, Ella and Lexi appeared. Each carried a plate covered with a silver dome.

"Dinner is served," Ella giggled. She leaned close to Zander and whispered, "You owe me." She placed her plate in front of him. When both plates were on the table she declared, "Bon appétit!" She lifted her cover. In unison, Ella and Lexi backed up in a move that seemed rehearsed and disappeared from sight.

She stared down at her plate. Lobster, seasoned rice, asparagus.

"You catered this? That's so sweet."

"No. I cooked this."

"You. Zander Bellamie cooked all this. I'm impressed."

"Don't be." He laughed. "It took me nine tries before I figured out how to get the lobster and rice perfect. Honestly, if I see lobster within the next six months ...." He groaned.

The sweet gesture touched her somewhere that hadn't been reached in a very long time. "Thank you, Zander. This is lovely."

"No. You are lovely. Thank you for being with me tonight."

She smiled at the compliment.

"How was your week?" He picked up his fork.

"Busy, but nice. I practiced a few pastries. New combinations I invented. The guests loved them. How about yours?" She frowned when his phone rang. He answered it and told whoever was on the other end he was busy and would call them back later.

He hung up and resumed their conversation. "My week was good. Little Red is healing nicely, and the kits are growing like weeds." Slowly the awkwardness that had started with their little spat faded away and they talked in earnest.

Four times he got text messages, responded to them, but didn't leave. She was impressed that he was taking her conditions seriously.

When they finished their main courses, he slipped into the house and came back with two small servings of strawberry shortcake. He placed them on the table with a flourish. "For you, my Canuck. Because you said Canadians like their strawberry shortcake."

"What a shame, I was craving that classic American apple pie." She winked.

"Next time. This meal was challenging enough."

She reached out and grasped his hand as he sat down. "Thank you for this. You went to a lot of trouble, and I appreciate it. It means a lot to me."

"You're very welcome."

His phone was blessedly silent for the rest of the night. She actually felt like their relationship was going well. She couldn't help the niggle of doubt that said all good things must come to an end.

Chapter 19

Two days later, Heather sat in one of the inn's Adirondack chairs overlooking the ocean and basked in the romantic glow of their dinner. She grinned as she worked on the menu for the inn's long weekend meals. She had already approved extra staff for the event. She'd need servers for both inside and outside as well as a couple of extra line chefs. It was early afternoon and the air was quite cool. She wrapped her shawl tighter and picked up her pen.

"Good morning, beautiful." Zander's voice came from behind her.

"Oh! You startled me. I didn't hear you over the waves and the seagulls." She smiled up at him. Good morning." King raced by to chase seagulls up and down the beach. He just ran from one to another barking without doing them any harm. They seemed to enjoy teasing him by flying close and swooping off again.

Zander handed her a steaming mug topped with whipped cream and bent to brush a kiss across her cheek before he sat in the white chair beside her. "Steaming mochaccino for a steaming woman." His wink went straight to her toes.

"Thank you!" She paused. "Did you talk to Derrick?" she asked. It still worried her that she might lose her job if things went bad between them. If her boss walked by and saw them kissing, there could be trouble.

"I talked to Derrick, Jacob, Lexi, Ella, my mother, my receptionist, and my assistant. They are all okay with this relationship going forward. Jeremy, on the other hand, wants you to dump me and date him."

"Oh my gosh!" She covered her face. "You asked him?"

"Not really no. I'm just yanking your chain. But it was clear from the second he set eyes on you that he wanted you for himself."

"Maybe for a moment. But once he believed you and I were together, he only flirted to annoy you. The moment you left; all flirting stopped." She grinned.

"You were funny. And cute. Your jealousy was flattering."

"Jealousy is not a nice quality."

"If jealousy goes overboard, it isn't good, that's for certain. But just a touch is nice. It showed that you care."

"It's him I don't trust. Not you."

His frown was adorable. "You have nothing to fear from Jeremy. He was the perfect gentleman."

"How about we talk about something else?" Zander growled.

She reached out and patted his hand. "Aside from his culinary skills, Jeremy is nothing to me."

"Good. I'd hate to have to fight him."

She laughed. "Oh dear. I've heard stories about your family and fighting. You patched up Jacob, who would patch you up?" She couldn't resist teasing him.

"Ha. Ha. Very funny. It would be Jeremy that needed stitches, not me." He flexed his muscles.

She giggled. "Why aren't you at work?" It was just after his usual lunch break.

"I stopped by to see if you'd like to go for dinner tonight." His smile was pure charm. On anyone else it would be just a smile. From Zander, it warmed her to her toes.

"Of course. I'd love to. But you could have texted me."

"But then I wouldn't get to see your beautiful face and steal a couple kisses."

He leaned over and kissed her so hard and deeply that she nearly dropped her mocha. The man had talented lips. "Mm. I'm glad you did." She clasped his hand and leaned back in her chair. There was something so incredibly warm and relaxing about sitting and watching the ocean while holding the hand of the man you loved. She could stay here forever.

Whoa! Love? Did she love him?

Her heart panicked for a second, and after a very long moment, settled down to enjoy the feeling. She did love him! But was it enough to go forward seriously? Was she ready for a long-term commitment? Was she jumping the gun? She told her mind to shut up and enjoy the feeling.

"I also had an ulterior motive for swinging by," he said quietly.

A gust of wind blew salty spray in her face. She sipped her drink and licked whipped cream off her lip before saying, "Oh? Should I be worried?"

"Maybe," he hedged. "I need a favor."

"Sure. What can I do?"

"Don't be so quick to agree." His pause was dramatic. "I need help on the long weekend. I'm working with the local shelter, Homes for Hounds. We're bringing batches of animals to the inn for adoption. We need more hands."

"I'm already cooking and serving. That's why I'm out here. I was planning my menu and organizing event staff. I'm not sure I have time for anything else. Sorry."

"Jacob and Derrick said the inn will pay for extra help in the kitchen for part of the day so you can come save some critters. It's one of their contributions to the event."

"The inn is hosting, providing electricity, giving tours. I'm prepping food for a fully booked inn. Three meals a day. I'm on the hook for cookies, cupcakes, and muffins. I'm not sure I can fit you in." Honestly, she didn't want to. She'd gradually adjusted to King being around but was still wary of him. But other dogs? Nope. Cats. Nope. She didn't want any part of that.

"I can't believe you'd even ask me," she said. "You know I'm terrified of cats and not a huge fan of dogs." King raced up the hill toward her, she reared back. He careened to a stop and dropped his head on her lap. Every muscle in her body went tense.

"King, sit," Zander commanded, and the massive beast dropped to his backside. "I know you're uncertain, but all the animals will be in pens. I need someone for paperwork and to accept donations. I've got a ton of high school kids to help with the animals. I need an adult for paperwork. You don't need to touch any animal."

That might be okay, but what if an animal got out? What if someone wanted her to hold their new pet. "I don't know ...."

"I swear, it will work out. Half the town is busy with this event. We want to put on a good show for the tourists. You're my last hope."

Ugh. The desperation card. Why did it feel so much like the guilt card? "Fine. But I'm not getting close to any animal. Paperwork only."

"Thank you." Gratitude rang in his words. "You won't regret it."

Somehow, she doubted that, but being in a relationship meant compromises and this cause was important to him.

His phone rang. He looked at her and winced before he answered it. "Hi, Mom." He was quiet for several minutes, though he did nod his head as if his mother could see him. Finally, he said, "I'll be right there. Bye, Mom."

He looked apologetic as he hung up. "I've got to run. Mom needs some stuff out of the attic." He paused with an odd look on his face, like he wanted to say something. He stood and patted his leg to get King's attention. "I'll pick you up at your place at seven, if that works for you."

"Fine." She didn't know how to ask if what his mother needed was important and knew the annoyance showed in her voice.

His look was quizzical, like he knew she wasn't fine. "Later then," he said after a long pause.

She stared at the ocean torn between being pleased that he came to visit her and being annoyed that he rushed off. His ulterior motive wasn't exactly heart touching either.

♥♥♥

"Guess what I scored," Zander bragged, excitement filling his voice.

"You won the lottery?" Heather teased.

"Guess again?"

"You hired a new vet to help out?" she asked hopefully. She fiddled with her silverware. Zander had been twitchy during the hour-long drive to Richmond, British Columbia. He was super excited. Teasing him was fun.

"Not yet, but I have several applications." He smiled. "Come on. Guess. It's something fun.

Something you'll want to do." He drummed his fingers on the table.

"We're going skydiving. I've always wanted to try that."

"What kind of idiot wants to jump out of a perfect good airplane?"

"I give up." She wasn't much for guessing games.

"I scored two tickets to Rio Del Bravo in concert in Vancouver. Tomorrow night." He pulled them from his shirt pocket and waved them at her.

"What?" She laughed. "No way! They are my all-time favorite group. Those boots and cowboy hats. Mmm. The lead singer's voice gives me chills. How did you get tickets? They were sold out months ago."

"Friend of a friend. I called in a few favors. Want to go with me?"

"I can't miss work." Her elation fled in a heartbeat.

"I've already okayed it with Derrick. Your assistant can cover for you. Come on. It's two days. A day to get there, the concert, and home the next day. One of those days is your day off."

"You went to my boss before you asked me?"

"Sure, why not? He's my brother. Family does favors for family. Easy peasy."

His breezy attitude irked her. He had no right to go behind her back like that. "We need a new rule," she said.

"Seriously?" He frowned. "I give you tickets of a lifetime, and you want new rules?" He sighed. "Fine. What rule do I have to abide by now?" he grumbled.

She counted to ten. "I'm an adult. I'm capable of asking for time off. Which I would gladly do to go to the concert with you. I don't like you running my life. Please, in the future, let me do the asking. Don't try to run my life."

"Is that the rule?" He sounded annoyed but resigned.

"Yes. Look. Marv liked to control every aspect of our relationship. Where we went and when. What we spent money on. I didn't know it at the time, but he was using me. Maybe I'm oversensitive about not being in charge." She knew it was a crappy explanation where an apology might be better, but it was all she had.

"I apologize if I overstepped. It won't happen again."

His brows pinched together, and his mouth turned down. He was upset by her lack of excitement and her new rule. Well, he could suck it. She was upset that he was trying to run her life. She'd ridden in that rodeo with Marv, and she wasn't saddling up again.

"Consider it forgotten." Again, a poor response, but still heartfelt.

"Heather, will you please accompany me to the concert?"

"Yes, Zander, I will go to the concert with you." His smile was like the sun breaking out from behind the clouds. She couldn't help but grin. She wiggled in her seat. "Oh my gosh! I can't believe you got those tickets. I'm super stoked."

"Oh gosh. I'll have to pack!"

"Can we eat first?" he teased.

She laughed. "Yes! I'm starving all of a sudden. This is amazing. Thank you!" She was giddy all through dinner and didn't even mind when he took five phone calls and answered a dozen texts. At least not until the waitress brought their dessert just as his phone rang again.

He held up a finger, halting the young woman in her tracks. "I'll be there as fast as I can." He turned to the server. "Can we get the bill and get those desserts to go? And two cups of coffee? Thanks."

The server looked at Heather. They both blinked in confusion. Heather shrugged. It must be important. "One black coffee, one with cream and sugar, please."

Before she knew it, they were speeding down the highway toward home. "What's wrong?" she asked.

"Tyson fell off a ladder."

"Oh my gosh! Is he badly hurt?" He must be if she judged by the speed Zander was going.

"Twisted his bum knee. Maybe broke it. I need to get him to the hospital." He did a quick shoulder check and flew out around the semi in front of them.

"What? What about your other brothers? Don't they drive?" she said sarcastically. "How about your mom. I know she drives. Couldn't one of them take him to the hospital?"

"He called me. My brother needs me and I'm going."

"You didn't answer me," she snapped. "What's wrong with the rest of your family. Or an ambulance. Half Moon Bay does have ambulances."

"He's my brother. He needs me. I'm going to him."

This was exactly what she feared would happen when she set down her ground rules. She understood if nobody else was available, and since he refused to state that they were, she suspected that Zander had been Tyson's first call. She sat and fumed. Maybe she was being over-sensitive, but the man had no boundaries with his family. They called and he ran, no matter what else he was involved in, and no matter how trivial their need. And this after he spent so much of their date on the phone with clients. Hadn't these people heard of office hours?

He tore past another vehicle coming way to close to an oncoming car.

"Slow down!" she yelled. "You won't do Tyson any good if you die on the way to play taxi." She hadn't meant to say the last part, but Zander didn't seem to notice it. He slowed down marginally in the area of the border crossing and sped up again once they cleared the checkpoint.

Before she knew it, he was at her curb, car in gear, engine running.

"Thanks for dinner," she said, not meaning it in the least.

"Ya. Ya. Pick you up at eight tomorrow morning." He reached over and pulled her door shut and roared away leaving her in a cloud of dust.

"Thanks for the lovely evening, Heather," she said to herself. "It was wonderful to spend quality time with you." She flipped the bird toward his retreating car. Jerk.

Chapter 20

By morning Heather had managed to put aside her anger at Zander. Both for going behind her back to ask Derrick if she could have the day off, and for dumping her to rush to his brother's aid. She knew he was trying to give her a nice date at the concert, and to make it easier by securing time off.

He was worried about his brother's leg too. If it made him rush to end the date, it was okay. Frustrating, but okay. Besides, she had promised to give him several chances. Though it seemed like he was fast using them up.

The test would start tonight. Could he spend two days with her without abandoning her for his family or clients? He really did need to hire another vet to fill in for him. Surely there were fresh grads looking for work.

She packed an overnight bag and grabbed her jacket. She was downstairs waiting for him at exactly eight. Two minutes later, he pulled up in his shining

Camaro. He hopped out and came around to her side of the car.

"Good morning, beautiful. You look lovely." He wrapped his arms around her and brushed his lips across hers.

"Good morning." Seeing his smile made the last of her tension slide away.

"Let me get that bag." He eased it from her fingers and opened her door for her. Once she was inside, he shut the door, and placed her bag in the trunk.

"Smells great in here," she said once he was inside and buckled up.

"Mocha in the short cup for you. Tall black coffee in the large for me. I didn't grab any food, I thought we'd stop for breakfast or brunch on the way. Do you still have your passport?"

"I do. Thanks for the coffee."

He rolled through town and in no time, they were on the highway heading north. The radio played soft jazz. The sun peeked through the clouds pretty and bright but not overly hot yet. Her cup was warm in her hand and her heart soared. Today was going to be a great day.

"How's Tyson's leg?" she asked half an hour after they hit the highway.

"Not broken thank heaven. Badly strained and some torn ligaments. He's pretty lucky."

"Did you get him to the hospital okay? No issues getting him into the car?"

"Yeah. About that. Derrick and Jacob called just after I dropped you off. Tyson called them and they got him to the hospital. I'm sorry I ditched our date."

"Apology accepted." It seemed like she was always accepting his apology for something. She pushed the negative thought aside. He did seem to be trying to focus on her. Today's tickets were proof of that. She decided to find the positive and make the best of the day.

♥♥♥

The concert was amazing. Both warmup bands were talented, and Heather purchased their CDs during the short break before the main act. The stadium was rocking. She was holding their beer as

265

they stood in line for burgers when Zander pulled his phone out.

"Derrick, what's up?"

Heather rolled her eyes. Hadn't he told his brother they were on a date out of town? It was a miracle he managed to call during intermission.

He made several sounds of agreement and a few grunts. "Okay. I'll head back. See you soon." He hung up.

"I beg your pardon?" Heather glared at him.

"Tyson's being airlifted to a hospital in Seattle. There's a bleed in his knee and they can't figure out why. He needs immediate surgery. We have to go. We need to get to the airport and find a flight to Seattle."

Heather counted to ten. Emergency surgery was a big deal, she understood that. But what good did leaving in the middle of the concert do? He couldn't help his brother at this point. He had two other brothers to take care of his mother.

"I think you mean you have to go," she snapped. "I'm not leaving. I came all this way to see a concert and I'm going to see it."

"Don't be ridiculous. He's my brother. He needs surgery." Zander's voice rose and the people around them turned to stare.

"I don't care. Rushing back won't help. He's taking a damned helicopter to the hospital. He'll be in surgery before you get there anyway. Leaving doesn't make sense. We're supposed to be on a date."

Some woman shouted, "You tell him, girl."

She glared at the woman.

"Come on, Heather. Don't be unreasonable."

"Think it through, Zander. He'll be out of surgery before you arrive. What's the rush? Why can't we finish our date?"

"He's my brother! That's it. I'm done," Zander shouted. "I'm done with your stupid rules. Family comes first. Always."

She slammed the plastic cups of beer into his chest. "Go. I'll find my own way home. Screw you and your entire family, Zander Bellamie. Screw you."

The crowd cheered as she stomped away.

Chapter 21

Heather flew into the washroom and collapsed against a stall wall. Tears streaked down her cheeks, and she sobbed.

"Are you okay in there?" someone asked.

She hiccupped. "I'm fine."

"You don't sound fine," the woman said softly.

"True." She laughed wryly. "I'm not. But I will be."

"Okay. If you're sure."

Clicking heels marked the woman's departure. Rio Del Bravo opened their part of the concert with their latest number one single and the crowd roared. Heather straightened her spine and wiped her tears. She'd driven over an hour to see this band and no stupid man was going to stop her. She pushed out of the stall, washed her hands, and rinsed her face with cold water.

The music was deafening as she left the restroom and made her way to her seat. She stood at the top of the stairs looking down, taking in the crowd, and the band's antics. Thousands of people held up their phones, some videoing, some with flashlights on pointed upward, mimicking lighters at 80s concerts. It was incredible. Their joy and energy flooded through her.

"Excuse me," a women said. Someone pushed against her back. She stepped to the side and looked at the people behind her.

"Marv?"

"Heather?" He stared at her for several seconds. "I've been trying to call you. I need a manager and you have great people skills. You're the perfect choice. Come work for me."

"No thanks." *Hell no!* "What are you doing here?" She could barely get her mind around the fact that he was at a concert so far from home. And offering a job to the woman you robbed, he had more gall than ten other men. *Idiot.*

"Came to see the band. They're not touring Toronto this time. How are you?" he asked as if he actually cared.

The charming smile that once enticed her left her cold. "I'm great, I've got an amazing gig as head chef for an inn just over the border."

"Enough of old home week." Marv's wife glared. "I want to see this concert." Her stomach was flat and lean, her pregnancy long passed. She surged forward pushing past Marv. She nudged Heather with her shoulder on her way by.

Heather teetered on the edge of the step. She felt herself going over backward. Her hand shot out and Marv reached for her. The space between their hands was too large and she flailed through the air. Her back hit something hard and she rolled over and over, somersaulting down the concrete stairs. Endless minutes later, she came to an abrupt halt against some seats. The crowd rushed her as everything went black.

Zander paced up and down the airway concourse. It was two hours until the next flight. He should have listened to Heather and stayed for the concert. His mother texted him every few minutes. There were no updates to report. Tyson had arrived at the hospital

271

and was in surgery. What he wouldn't give to be able to transport himself to his brother's side, or back at the concert with Heather.

His phone rang and he pulled it out. The number was unfamiliar. "Dr. Bellamie," he answered.

"Zander? This is Quinn."

"Quinn, hi." What did Heather's roommate want? "What can I do for you? Do you have a pet emergency? I'm out of town."

"No. But Heather's in the hospital."

His heart stopped and he gasped. "What?"

"She's in Vancouver. I thought you were with her at the concert. Something happened. She's got a broken leg and is all banged up. I'm her emergency contact. She didn't ask, but I think she needs you."

"What hospital?" he asked, sprinting toward the exit.

In an eerie reenactment of his two flights to save Tyson, he flew down the road toward Vancouver General, his GPS guiding his path. Traffic was blessedly light but still stop and go. With every red light and car he passed, he cursed himself for leaving her alone. She'd been right. There was nothing he could do for Tyson. But there was something he could do for Heather. He could be there.

What if she was hurt worse than Quinn said? What if she was seriously injured? He'd die! This was all his fault.

He roared into the hospital parkade and rushed inside. After a brief clash at reception, he stood at the desk of the emergency unit. "Where can I find Heather Olsen?" he asked the first nurse he encountered.

"Are you family?" The gray-haired woman asked.

"Yes," he lied.

She gave him a squinty look. "And you are ...?"

"Dr. Zander Bellamie." He added his title without clarifying that he was a veterinarian.

"Your names don't match. Look sir, I've been doing this job a long time. I know when I'm being hoodwinked. She's with the police. Take a seat."

"The police?" he almost screeched.

"Take a seat." Nurse Crabby jabbed her finger toward an overcrowded waiting room. "Now. Or I'll have security remove you from the hospital." She scowled. "Don't make me say it twice."

He nodded and walked away. Unable to sit still, he paced circles around the rows of chairs. A baby cried and was soothed by his mother. A man coughed over and over while his wife murmured encouraging phrases. A teenage girl wept and clutched her arm to her chest. This place was hell.

The stench of antiseptic, stale urine, and body odor crowded his nose until he wanted to gag. He rushed outside into the night air, hoping to dispel the feeling. He gasped and leaned against the dusty hospital exterior. After a moment, the nausea passed. He'd be fine if he could just see Heather. He went back inside. The desk was unoccupied. Looking left and right for staff, he crept past the desk and snuck down the hallway.

He paused outside each curtained alcove to listen. Finally, he heard her voice. "Heather?" he called out.

"Zander?" she responded just as Nurse Crabby shouted at him, "You! I said to wait in the waiting room. Get out of here. Before I call security."

The curtain opened and a smiling nurse stood there. "Zander, I presume?" she asked.

"Yes. Where's Heather?"

"In here."

"Zander, come in," Heather said, her voice sounding funny. The nurse waved him inside where the biggest RCMP officer he'd ever seen stood scowling beside Heather's bed.

Zander stepped toward Heather and stopped cold. He gasped. "Jeez," he whispered. "What the hell happened?" He rushed to her side.

Her face was black and blue, her head swaddled in a large bandage, her left leg was in an inflatable cast. He closed his eyes and swallowed away the pain stabbing at him. This happened because he abandoned her.

"I'm so sorry," he whispered. He stroked the back of her unbruised right hand.

"Not your fault." Her voice was garbled.

"Can we continue?" the officer demanded. "Sir, can you sit?" It wasn't a question.

Heather patted the bed, and he perched on the edge beside her, careful not to jostle her. He held her hand.

"Okay," the cop said, "Let's go over it one more time."

"I'm pretty sure it was an accident. I was at the concert," her voice shook and was almost unintelligible through the swelling in her face. "I was late going in."

"Why was that?"

Heat crept up Zander's face even as Heather's cheeks started to flush. "Because I just broke up with my boyfriend and he left me there."

The cop scowled. "This yahoo?" His voice was heavy with danger.

"Guilty," Zander said.

"You sure you want him here?"

"Yes." She winced and went on. "I was watching on the landing, waiting for the break between songs to head to my seat. I ran into someone I know. Or rather he ran into me. His wife pushed past me and the next thing I knew I was going backwards. I woke up here."

"And this guy's name?"

She told him.

"What the hell is he doing here?" Zander demanded. "Doesn't he live halfway across the country?"

"Sir. If you can't be quiet, I'll have to ask you to leave."

Heather squeezed his hand in hers and he mimed zipping his lip.

"They're from Ontario. Came out for the concert." She stretched toward the bedside table and winced.

"What do you need?" Zander asked.

"Wa'er," she mumbled.

He passed her the glass, and she sipped carefully before handing it back. The cop resumed his questions. They went on and on, and eventually satisfied, he sat and wrote out a statement. "Read this and sign it if it is accurate." He passed it to Heather. She read through the two-page report twice and scrawled her name at the bottom. "I've got your information. I'll be in touch once we talk to these people."

"I don't want to press charges," she said.

"You may not have a choice. In cases like this, the RCMP may choose to do it on your behalf. I'll let you know. Have a good night."

"Oh, Heather. I'm so sorry. I never should have left you there."

"I should have gone with you." Her crooked smile crushed him. "Zander, I was wrong. Family is important. I realized that as soon as you left. I should have gone after you. I knew where we parked."

"My fault. You were right. There's nothing I can do until Ty's surgery is finished. I was pacing at the airport waiting for a flight when Quinn called. You should have called me," he chided, stroking his finger down her arm. He had to touch her. He couldn't keep from reassuring himself that she was okay. Well, not okay exactly ... but going to be okay.

Heather smiled at his soft touch. It was exactly what she needed. His smile erased her earlier hurt feelings. He'd come back for her. He'd put her first! Her grin morphed until her swollen cheek hurt. "Thanks for coming back."

"How could I not? I love you, Heather Olsen." His smile warmed her heart. It felt full to bursting.

"I love you to Vancouver and back," he whispered then leaned forward and rested his forehead against hers and closed his eyes.

She closed hers to savor the moment. "I love you, Zander Bellamie." Being there, with him, was bliss. If it weren't for the agony of her injuries, this would be the perfect moment.

"Rio Del Bravo is playing in Abilene next month. Wanna go?" he asked.

Okay, maybe it was the perfect moment.

They sat quietly, holding hands without speaking until after one final check, Heather was discharged. "Have her take one of the anti-inflammatories every six hours. Don't let her skip one. They work best stacked," Nurse Crabby said. "She needs rest. Have her family doctor check on that leg in a week." She handed him a paper. "Read this. Watch for the signs mentioned and if you think anything is wrong, anything at all, take her to the nearest emergency department. The hospital will send her a bill."

"I'm right here," she grumbled.

They loaded her into a wheelchair and an orderly pushed her to the car. They spent three days in adjoining rooms in The Fairmont Pacific Rim Hotel in Vancouver. Zander pampered her every second. The meds made her sleepy and she spent more time asleep than awake.

Wednesday, she woke up feeling semi-human and almost refreshed. "Zander?" She knocked on the door between their rooms though it was ajar. "Are you there?"

"Sure am." The door opened and he leaned against the jamb and smiled down at her. "You look better."

"I feel better."

"Excellent." He leaned toward her; his gaze fixed on her mouth. "Good enough for a kiss?" he whispered.

"Definitely." She braced herself on the doorframe and lifted up as best she could. She needed him close. Their lips brushed once, feather light. And again. And again. He stepped back.

"As much as I'd like to continue this line of action. I think it's best left for after you are healed."

She whimpered, just a little. "Okay." She wrapped her arms around his waist and leaned into him, savoring the solid feel of his body, and of his heart beating against hers. "How's Tyson?" She asked the same question every morning.

"He's good. He'll be home in time for the celebration. Speaking of which ...." he stepped back and looked down at her, love filling his eyes.

"I have staff to organize," she said. "I hope you'll forgive me if I bail on your animal event. I don't want to hang out in public with this face." She waved at herself. "I think I'll confine myself to the kitchen."

"I thought so. I've hired a new veterinarian. I interviewed him online yesterday while you slept. He starts tomorrow. He'll help with Homes for Hounds."

"Thank you." She leaned into him for another minute before dragging herself away to pack her few belongings.

Epilogue

Half of Heather wanted to hide inside the kitchen. Her bruises were horrendous. Her legs were black and blue, so were her arms. She had a string of seven stitches across her forehead and her entire face was purple fading to yellow. But she had said she'd work with Homes for Hounds, and she would.

They'd gotten home on Wednesday. She had hoped for some quiet time at home, but realistically, it wasn't feasible. The festival started Thursday. She had a kitchen to organize and food to prep.

Their first stop after leaving the city was the inn. They pulled up out front, and Zander's family had rushed out. Even Tyson hobbled out on his crutches. She buried her face in her hands. "I can't do this. I look awful."

Zander brushed his hand down her hair so softly she barely felt it. "Look at me, Heather."

She peeked up at him. Having him see her wretched state wasn't so awful. He'd been there from the start. But showing her bruises to the public was more than she could handle at that moment.

"You don't look awful." She gave him an "are you nuts," look. "Okay, maybe you do. But it's through no fault of your own. If anyone should feel bad, it's me. I left you there. If I had stayed, we'd have been seated and you never would have been on those stairs to bump into Marv. You'd be uninjured."

"Oh, Zander. This isn't your fault. We fought. Everyone fights. I hate it and I don't want to do it again, but I'm sure we will." She paused. "What was I saying? Oh. Ya. Not your fault, not my fault. But I look terrible."

"You look beautiful in purple and yellow." He deadpanned.

She couldn't help but laugh at the ridiculous comment. "Gee. Thanks." She sighed. "Guess I'll face the music." She climbed out of the car and Ella rushed to her side.

"Slow down, munchkin," Zander warned. "She's the walking wounded."

Ella stopped dead. "Are you okay? You look terrible."

"Ella!" Her father chided.

"Well, she does, but she looks cool too."

"I'll have some scars to show off later, won't I." She greeted everyone and accepted their condolences on her condition. "I appreciate all the support; it means a lot."

"You're family," Beth said. "Bellamies support each other. Come on, I've got tea and snacks ready in the dining room."

"You made snacks?" Zander teased his mom.

"I didn't say that. I said I had them ready. Why would I try and bake when there's a perfectly good kitchen staff with way more talent than I have?" She took Heather by the arm and led her inside. The inn was cool after the blazing sun outside and it smelled deliciously of sweet baked goods. Beth led her to the dining room.

"Wow, this looks amazing." Heather stared at the table. Full tea and coffee service was laid on the sideboard and the table was covered in sweets.

285

Cinnamon rolls, four kinds of cookies, muffins, cupcakes, mini apple pies, and individual strawberry shortcakes. The table was draped in a white linen cloth with pretty blue plates and cups and saucers. It was fit for high tea. "Thanks for this."

Her sous chef came out of the kitchen. "Heather, good to have you back."

"Billy, it's good to be back. Did I miss anything? Where are we at with the preparations for the celebration?"

"Oh no you don't," Zander warned in unison with his brother Derrick.

"Tea first," Zander ordered. "Then you can dive in. Sit here." He led her to the head of the table and helped her sit. She was still achingly stiff and sore. Her bruised back was the worst. "Now," he said, "take one of these before you do anything else. You have to be sore from the trip." He passed her the prescription bottle.

"Thanks. I'm okay. I don't like it; it muddles my head. I need a clear head to work."

"Take it," he ordered. "Nurse Crabby said you need to keep taking it."

"Who's Nurse Crabby," Ella asked.

"I was in the hospital, in emerg, and my roommate called Zander."

"And I rushed to her aid, leaving my favorite brother to fend for himself in the hospital," Zander declared.

"Suck it," Tyson said. "I didn't need you, I had Mom."

"Anyway," Zander went on, ignoring Tyson. "I got there and because I wasn't family, Nurse Crabby wouldn't even let me in. So, I waited until she was busy." He paused dramatically. "And I snuck past her to find Heather. There was this big burly Canadian cop ...." he went on to over dramatize the whole time he was at the hospital.

Everyone listened with different degrees of skepticism.

"So, you save her again, like you did with the cat!" Ella exclaimed. "That's so cool. You're like a knight in shining armor."

"He's more like a knight in battered tinfoil," Heather said. "But he's okay."

He nudged the meds toward her. In the end, she settled for some over-the-counter pain relief and a big cup of lemon raspberry tea.

Zander snuck a glance at Heather where she sat behind a folding table, under a pop-up tent, and talked to the proud new parents of a teacup poodle. He moved closer so he could watch her. Lord, he couldn't get enough of staring at her. Her every action brought a smile to his face.

"Here you go," she handed the couple a gift certificate to Tweets and Growls Pet Shop. Every family adopting a pet over the weekend received one. "Let me get you some information." She organized a folder with pet care instructions, the vet clinic's information, and dog training schools in the area. "This should be everything you need."

"Thanks so much. We're going to love Oscar," the woman gushed.

"He's certainly adorable," she said, sounding sincere. "Don't forget that even though we've waived our usual adoption fee for the weekend, we're still taking donations for the shelter."

The woman looked at her husband and he pulled out his wallet. He dropped a hundred dollars in the donation jar. Heather stood and shook his hand. She might not be enamored with pets, but Heather sure knew how to get people to donate. She'd raised more money today than the shelter had in months. Several families offered to pay the usual adoption fee and made a donation while they talked to her.

"Thank you so much. We really appreciate that. All the pets do."

As the couple wandered away, Ella walked up.

"Hi, Heather," his niece said. She slipped a small, covered basket on the table.

"You look happy. What's in the basket? Can I peek?"

"Um. You better not," Ella said.

Zander knew what the basket held. He'd been waiting for this moment. He walked up to the table. "Can I see?" he asked.

"You don't need to see; you know what it is." Ella declared.

"What's the big secret?" Heather asked. The basket made a squeaking sound, and she jerked back. "Is there an animal in there?"

Ella giggled. "Yes."

"It must be pretty small. Is it a mouse? A hamster? A guinea pig? Oh, I know," she declared, "it's a chicken."

Ella roared with laughter. Zander smiled. Heather was amazing with his niece.

"Let me show you," Zander said. He picked up the basket and walked to the side of the table. "Come close." Heather gave him a wary look but shifted toward him.

"I'm not going to like this, am I?" She asked.

Ella giggled. "It's okay, Heather."

Heather looked back and forth between Ella and Zander. Something was up. "Should I be afraid?"

"No," Zander said. "You should be happy." His smile warmed her to her toes.

"Okay, if you're sure." What could possibly be in the basket? A tiny meow came from between the wicker rings of the basket. "I get it. It's a kitten." She inhaled deeply. How bad could it be? The basket was small. That meant the kitten was small too. Right?

She straightened her spine and got ready to jump in case it attacked.

Zander set the basket on her lap and opened the lid. She leaned away, just in case.

A tiny, wee black and white kitten looked up at her, its eyes sleepy. It yawned and made a little meep sound.

"Oh, it's adorable."

"You can pet it," Elle enthused.

After confirming with Zander, she reached out to touch it. The kitten stretched up to meet her fingers. "Oh. It's so soft." When it stretched, she noticed it had a ribbon collar around its neck with something dangling from it.

"Do you want to hold it?" Zander asked.

291

She hesitated. She'd been brave enough to trust Zander with fake dating, then real dating, and he'd come through for her when she really needed him. Could she trust him now? Could she be brave enough to reach past her fear of animals?

"Okay. I guess." The kitten was much smaller than the one that had attacked her decades ago. How much damage could it possibly do?

He set the kitten on her lap. It purred and snuggled against her.

"Oh, it's adorable. And not mean at all."

"Most cats aren't. Unless they're wild." Zander rubbed the kitten's back.

She stroked its head and scratched its ears. "What its name?" She turned the ribbon collar looking for a tag. It spun a shiny gold ring right into her hand. "What's this?" She looked at Zander. He was down on one knee in front of her.

"Heather Olsen, I know we've only known each other for weeks. You've taught me so much about myself, and about setting boundaries. I've learned that my family is more than capable of looking after themselves, thanks to you. I couldn't imagine having time to date until you came along."

She wrinkled her nose at him, and he tapped it with his finger.

"I'm not finished. You asked for friendship, I offered fake dating. I thought it would keep my heart safe. I was wrong. So very, very wrong. I fell in love with you. No, I fell deeper in love with you. I'm certain I fell for you the moment I saw you serving hors d'oeuvres at the inn's opening. The sun was glinting off your hair and you looked like an angel. I love you, more than I ever imagined I could love another person. Heather, will you marry me?"

With every word he spoke, her heartbeat accelerated until it pounded in her ears. Her chest grew tight. She gasped. "Yes. Yes. Yes." She wanted to fling her arms around him, but the cat had dozed off on her lap.

"Um, I want to hug you, but the cat ...."

He slipped his hand under the kitten and passed it to Ella who placed it back into the basket. "I'll take that kiss now," he teased.

She flung herself into his arms and pressed her lips against his. Electricity danced over her skin making her feel alive. She poured all her love into the kiss and felt his in his embrace. They kissed until the cheering crowd penetrated.

"Oh." She giggled.

"Are you going to keep the kitten?" Ella intruded.

Heather looked from the kitten to Zander and back. "I think maybe I will. He doesn't seem so scary."

"It's a girl," Ella declared.

"Well then, I think I'll keep her.

"You should call her Narwhal," Ella exclaimed.

"You can't name a cat Narwhal," Zander declared.

Heather took the kitten back and cuddled it to her cheek and neck. "I'm living in an ocean town; she needs an ocean name. She's mine, I'll call her whatever I want, and I want to call her Narwhal."

Ella giggled.

Zander laughed and slipped his arm around her waist. She leaned into him as a sense of perfect peace and contentment washed over her. This was exactly where she was meant to be.

♥♥♥

Did you enjoy Zander and Heather's story?
Please leave a review at your favorite retailer.

The Bellamie Brothers of Half Moon Bay is a four-book sweet small-town romance series comprised of connected but standalone stories written by Katie O'Connor and Audrey Carnes.

Watch for the rest of this heartwarming series.

Book 3: *Derrick's story. (title coming soon)*
Derrick and Sammi's story in the summer of 2023.

Book 4: *Playing for Keeps in Half Moon Bay*
Tyson and Quinn will follow in the fall of 2023.

If you haven't already, check out Book1:
The Billionaire Innkeeper of Half Moon Bay
and discover Lexi and Jacob's sweet story.

Up Next:

Derrick's Story
Audrey Carnes

He's her brother's best friend that she's always been in love with…

Sammi's had a crush on Derrick, the handsome, brooding, and most tempestuous of the Bellamie Brothers, since middle school. Five years ago, he made all of her childhood dreams come true with a single kiss in her family's restaurant, but treated her like a stranger the very next day. It's time for her to stop hanging onto old hopes and find someone who can truly love her back…except now Derrick needs her help.

Five years ago, Derrick made the mistake of a lifetime and kissed his best friend's little sister. She's gorgeous and smart–too good for him then and still too good for him now. But with the chef at his inn out for a few days, he needs Sammi's help to feed the guests more than scrambled eggs and protein shakes.

Will working together force them to admit their feelings for each other or will they go their separate ways? Find out in this sweet romance about family, love, and second chances!

About Katie O'Connor

Best-selling author Katie O'Connor lives in Calgary, Alberta, Canada. She married her high school sweetheart and is living her happily ever after. She is the mother of two grown daughters and is extremely proud of her five grandchildren.

She is the founder of The Write Chicks, a private romance writers' group set up with the sole purpose of supporting each other's writing career. Currently she is the chapter president of the Calgary branch of the Romance Writers of America and head of their mentoring group. In the past, she's been their secretary and has also served on the organizing committee for When Words Collide, a reader and writer conference in Calgary, Alberta.

Katie's career path has been long and twisted, with most of her life devoted to her family. She's been a waitress, chambermaid, cashier, store manager, as well as a lab and X-ray technician. She's been a small business owner and is an avid quilter and crafter.

She's dabbled in writing since high school because something drives her to create stories. She swears it's impossible for her NOT to write. Unsatisfied with one genre, Katie writes contemporary romance, fantasy/paranormal romance, and romantic suspense. Her favorite genre is sweet small-town contemporary.

She believes in all things magical, including dragons, fairies, UFOs, ghosts, and house pixies. But most of all she believes in love, romance, and hope.

Katie's Social Links

Email: katie@katieohwrites.com
Mailchimp Signup: http://eepurl.com/Q2nRr
Website: https://katieohwrites.com
Facebook: http://www.facebook.com/katieohwrites
Bookbub: https://www.bookbub.com/profile/katie-o-connor
Link Tree: https://linktr.ee/katieohwrites